Georgina smiled w to make one more said when Langsto open A Stitch at a Time in early July.

"Congratulations, sweetheart. Are you ready to celebrate?"

"Not yet. I'm going to wait for my grand opening."

"Have you eaten?"

"No. Why?"

"I know I can't keep you out too late, so I'm coming over to take you to the Den. Once you're up and running, I'll take you someplace real fancy so we can celebrate on a grand scale."

Georgina wanted to tell Langston that she didn't need a fancy restaurant to commemorate what she'd planned and patiently waited for. The fact that her shop was going to become a reality was enough. However, it had been a while since she'd gone to the sports bar. The last time was when Sutton had come up from Atlanta during the All Star break. When they'd walked in together he'd been given the rock-star treatment with fist bumps, slaps on the back and some had even asked for his autograph.

"Give me time to shower and change my clothes."

"Can you be ready in thirty minutes?"

She glanced at the clock on the microwave. It was seven thirty. "Yes."

"I'll be there at eight."

WICKHAM FALLS WEDDINGS:
Small-town heroes, bighearted love!

Dear Reader,

I sincerely want to thank you for your ongoing support for the Wickham Falls Weddings series, and welcome you back to a town with quirky folks who will occasionally remind you of members in your own family.

You caught a glimpse of Georgina Powell in *Second-Chance Sweet Shop*, and once she appeared on page I knew I wanted to know more about this biracial beauty who has become a modern-day Cinderella.

In *Starting Over in Wickham Falls*, Langston has returned after an award-winning career as a foreign correspondent covering wars on the other side of the world to assume ownership of a failing biweekly. As the editor in chief of *The Sentinel*, he is involved in civic and governmental affairs, and when he is seated at the same table with Georgina during a fund-raiser dinner-dance, he finds himself enchanted with the stunningly beautiful thirtysomething woman who still lives with her parents.

Georgina, who has deferred her dream to become an illustrator to join her family's business, is drawn to the erudite journalist who supports her ambition to join the ranks of a growing number of the town's independent businesswomen. What begins as an easygoing friendship evolves into a relationship as she discovers herself falling in love with a man who doesn't view her as just the heiress to the town's most profitable business enterprise.

Happy reading!

Rochelle Alers

Starting Over
in Wickham Falls

———

ROCHELLE ALERS

HARLEQUIN
SPECIAL
EDITION

Recycling programs
for this product may
not exist in your area.

ISBN-13: 978-1-335-89455-7

Starting Over in Wickham Falls

Copyright © 2020 by Rochelle Alers

All rights reserved. No part of this book may be used or reproduced in
any manner whatsoever without written permission except in the case of
brief quotations embodied in critical articles and reviews.

This is a work of fiction. Names, characters, places and incidents
are either the product of the author's imagination or are used fictitiously.
Any resemblance to actual persons, living or dead, businesses,
companies, events or locales is entirely coincidental.

This edition published by arrangement with Harlequin Books S.A.

For questions and comments about the quality of this book,
please contact us at CustomerService@Harlequin.com.

Harlequin Enterprises ULC
22 Adelaide St. West, 40th Floor
Toronto, Ontario M5H 4E3, Canada
www.Harlequin.com

Printed in U.S.A.

Since 1988, national bestselling author **Rochelle Alers** has written more than eighty books and short stories. She has earned numerous honors, including the Zora Neale Hurston Award, the Vivian Stephens Award for Excellence in Romance Writing and a Career Achievement Award from *RT Book Reviews*. She is a member of Zeta Phi Beta Sorority, Inc., Iota Theta Zeta Chapter. A full-time writer, she lives in a charming hamlet on Long Island. Rochelle can be contacted through her website, www.rochellealers.org.

Chapter One

Georgina Powell stared at her reflection in the full-length mirror, shocked and saddened at the same time with her transformation. The last time she'd taken special care with her appearance was for her high school prom. And that had been more than a decade ago. What, she asked herself, had she been doing for the past fourteen years? But she knew the answer; she hadn't been living but just existing.

Her dream of enrolling in art school to become an illustrator had vanished completely with the unexpected death of her thirteen-year-old brother from meningitis. Her parents had been planning for Kevin to take over running the store once they retired, but their plans were transferred to her.

Kevin's death changed their family's dynamics. Her mother appeared emotionally unable to recover from losing a child; her father threw himself into running the business as if it was a startup instead of one that had been well established for generations. And it had taken Georgina a very long time to come to the realization that her brother, whom she'd nicknamed Shadow because he followed her around as if he feared she would disappear, was gone and wasn't coming back.

Tonight signaled a change in Georgina's life. Not only did she look different outwardly, but she'd also changed inwardly. The body-hugging black gown and matching four-inch, silk-covered stilettos had replaced the ubiquitous navy blue smock with Powell's Department Store stitched over the back she wore over dark slacks. Her face with smoky shadows on her lids and a vibrant vermilion lip color, curly hair flat-ironed and tucked into a twist behind her ear completed her outward makeover. But it was her determination to move out of the house where she'd lived for the past thirty-two years that would alter her life.

Once her father downsized, and then eliminated the arts and crafts area of the store in order to expand the sporting goods section, it sparked an idea that had nagged at her for weeks. Georgina boxed up the stock and dropped it off at a storage facility with the intent of establishing her own business in the same town where she'd spent her entire life.

Picking up a black silk-lined cashmere shawl trimmed in faux fox, to ward off the chill of the mid-March night air, an envelope with the invitation and a beaded evening bag, Georgina walked out of the bedroom and down the back staircase to the garage located behind the two-story house. She managed to leave without encountering her mother. This was to become her first Wickham Falls Chamber of Commerce fund-raiser, an event that had been supported by both parents over the years, and then by only her father following Kevin's passing.

Georgina was shocked one night when after closing, Bruce Powell informed her that he wouldn't be attending and that she should take his place to represent the business. And when she'd asked her father why, his comeback was that it was time for her to prepare to take complete control of the department store once he retired. She'd wanted to tell him that she had no intention of managing the store because if she was going to assume that type of responsibility then it would be her own business enterprise.

She slipped behind the wheel of her late-model Nissan Rogue, an SUV she'd purchased to celebrate her thirty-second birthday. And at the beginning of the year, she'd made a New Year's resolution to cross off at least three of the remaining nine notations on her to-do list. The first had been to trade in the Mini

Cooper for the Rogue because she needed more room to transport the items needed to stock her new store.

Georgina started up the vehicle that still claimed a new-car smell and headed for the venue in Wickham Falls where the fund-raiser would be held for the first time. In the past the members of the Chamber had contracted with a hotel off the interstate to hold the annual event in one of their ballrooms.

A shiver of excitement rippled through Georgina when she thought about the plans she'd made for her future. She was aware that she had to work hard and probably make unforeseen sacrifices to realize her dream to become an independent business owner. But the knowledge that she would join a small number of women owning and operating their own businesses in Wickham Falls, West Virginia, was heady indeed.

Fifteen minutes later she maneuvered into a space between a Ram 1500 and a Ford F-150. *You can take the boy out of the country, but you can't take the country out of the boy*, she mused. Whether attending the local sports bar or a semiformal affair, pickups were the preferred modes of transportation in the town where the population still hovered below five thousand.

Thankfully, the Gibsons, who owned the Wolf Den, when they erected a barn at the rear of the property for larger gatherings, had paved the parking lot.

Georgina gathered her belongings off the passenger seat and alighted from the SUV.

A small crowd had gathered at the entrance to the barn and as she waited in line, she recognized several customers who patronized the department store. Powell's, as the locals called it, had survived despite big-box stores going up in neighboring towns because the Falls' town officials insisted if its citizenry lived local, then they should shop local. The town council had repeatedly voted down any developer's bid to put up strip malls with fast food restaurants and variety shops because they would impact and threaten the viability of Wickham Falls' mom-and-pop stores.

She finally made her way to the reception desk where the wives of several members were checking off names against ticket numbers. The woman glanced at her ticket, and then up at Georgina, her eyes widening in shock.

"Oh, my dear," she whispered. "I almost didn't recognize you, Georgina."

She gave the elderly woman with stylishly salt-and-pepper coiffed hair a sweet smile. "There are occasions when we're forced to clean up, Mrs. Bachmann."

The woman, whose husband was the Chamber's treasurer, nodded. "And I must say you clean up very well. I'm sorry your father can't attend, but I'm glad you're here to represent Powell's. By the way, you're at table number seven with others who will attend without a plus-one. You'll find your place card there."

"Thank you."

She wanted to tell the woman that Bruce Powell was upset that he'd had to attend another social event without his wife, which led to rumors that he and Evelyn were having marital issues. There wasn't an issue but that Evelyn Powell had become a social recluse. She was rarely seen in the store and had resigned from all the town's civic organizations. Even after sixteen years, Evelyn still mourned the loss of her son. Georgina would occasionally remind her that she did have a daughter, but the older woman ignored her as if she hadn't spoken.

She glanced around the barn that was reminiscent of a bygone era with strings of tiny white lights around the perimeter of the ceiling while gaslight-inspired chandeliers and hanging fixtures cast a warm, golden glow over round tables with seating for six. And in keeping with the theme of the time period of the early twentieth century, the glass, flatware and ornately carved mahogany bar added to the venue's rustic ambiance. White-jacketed waitstaff circulated with trays of hors d'oeuvres and flutes of champagne. Georgina draped her shawl over the back of one of the chairs at table seven.

"Georgi Powell, long time no see."

She turned to find Langston Cooper standing a

few feet away, holding a glass with an amber liquid, the color an exact match for his eyes, grinning at her. The orbs in a light brown complexion reminded her of champagne diamonds. Her attention was drawn to the minute lines fanning out around the eyes of the man who wasn't much older than she was. Langston had left Wickham Falls to attend college and had spent most of his career as a foreign journalist covering wars in Africa and the Middle East. She'd always thought of him as good-looking with his balanced features and a hint of a cleft in his strong chin, but there was something about Langston's body language that communicated he was so tightly coiled that people had to walk on eggshells in his presence.

"I could say the same about you," she countered, smiling. "Are you here as a member or as a reporter for the paper?"

Langston's eyebrows lifted slightly. "Both. Well, as editor-in-chief of *The Sentinel*, I'm expected to attend this soiree. What I don't remember is you coming last year."

"That's because this is my first year."

To say he was surprised to see Georgina at the event did not match his shock in seeing her wearing something other than the smock that identified her as an employee of Powell's Department Store. But then he had to remember she wasn't an employee but the daughter of the owner. He knew staring was rude, yet he couldn't pull his gaze away from her beautiful face with a subtle hint of makeup. However, it was the décolletage on the black halter gown that made it almost impossible for him not to stare at the soft swell of breasts each time she took a breath.

Mixed-race Georgina had inherited the best physical attributes from her Scotch-Irish father and African American mother. She'd concealed the faint sprinkling of freckles with makeup that was perfect for her light brown complexion. The brown curly hair with glints of copper were missing, and in its place was a sleek hairstyle that made her appear quite the sophisticate. When he'd returned to Wickham Falls the year before to purchase the failing periodical and encountered Georgina, the first thing he'd noticed was she no longer had the noticeable gap between her front teeth. He had always thought her pretty, but tonight she was stunning!

"Is there something I can get for you from the bar?"

She glanced at the waiters with the bubbly wine. "I'll have champagne. Meanwhile, I'm going to see what they're serving at the carving station, because if I'm going to drink, then I need to eat something."

Langston pulled out the chair with her shawl. "Please sit and I'll get you something to eat and your wine. How do you like your meat cooked?" He removed his suit jacket and placed it over the back of the chair next to hers.

She sat, smiling up at him. "Medium-well. Thank you, sir."

He returned her smile. "You're welcome, ma'am."

Langston approached a waiter. Reaching into the pocket of his suit trousers, he took out a money clip and handed the man a bill. "Can you please leave a couple of flutes at table seven?"

The young man pocketed the money, nodding. "Of course. And thank you, sir."

He wended his way through the crowd to the carving station, chiding himself for not telling Georgina that she looked incredible but did not want to come on too strong, because he didn't know if she was involved with someone. Just because she'd come unescorted, it did not translate into her being unencumbered. After all, she was a beautiful woman and heir to a successful business that had survived for decades despite the Great Depression and several recessions to remain viable.

Langston expertly balanced plates along his arm, a skill he'd learned when waiting tables as a college student. When he'd asked the waiter to leave a couple of flutes at the table, he hadn't meant a couple each for him and Georgina.

She pointed to the quartet of glasses. "He must have assumed we were thirsty," she teased.

He set down small plates with thinly sliced roast beef and horseradish, pasta with a vodka sauce, prawns with an Asian-inspired dipping sauce, and filo tartlets filled with spicy cilantro shrimp. "I'm willing to bet we'll need them because what I've selected for us definitely isn't bland."

Unfolding her napkin, Georgina spread it over her lap. "Spicy is good."

Langston gave her a sidelong glance. "So you like it hot?"

She nodded. "I enjoy a little heat," she admitted, spreading a smidgen of horseradish on the roast beef. "Do you cook?"

Her question caught him completely off guard. "I can. Why did you ask?"

Georgina shrugged bare shoulders. "Just curious."

Langston waited for her to chew and swallow a mouthful of meat. "What else are you curious about?"

"How is the paper doing since you took over?"

He successfully concealed his disappointment because he'd expected her to ask him something more personal—perhaps why he had come without a date. "It's taken a while, but we've managed to increase the circulation and advertising revenue."

"There was a time before you bought the paper that we thought it was going to fold. We've always relied on *The Sentinel* to advertise the store's daily and weekly specials."

"Powell's has advertised with the paper from its inaugural issue."

"It's the only way we can get the word out when we put items on sale."

Langston speared a prawn, dipped it into the piquant sauce and popped it into his mouth. "Do you find it odd that the Gibsons would offer an eclectic menu for the cocktail hour when they're known for barbecuing meat?"

The owners of the Wolf Den had established a reputation over several generations of serving the best grilled, barbecue and smoked meats in Johnson County. Longtime residents had whispered about the Gibsons keeping them supplied with illegal moonshine during Prohibition, and that revenue agents couldn't offer anyone enough money to snitch on their supplier. What went on in Wickham Falls stayed in Wickham Falls, and it was the reason he'd come back to his hometown to start over rather than remain in Washington, DC.

"They are full of surprises," Georgina said. "I suppose for catered affairs they like to change it up a bit."

"I really like the change."

"So do I," she agreed. "If this place had been up when we had prom, then we probably wouldn't have had to pay as much for our tickets or to contend with a power outage and a malfunctioning generator."

"My parents told me about that fiasco when they came up to New York for my college graduation."

"Some of the kids were talking about wrecking

the place when we were told we weren't getting a re-fund because the contract stated the owners weren't responsible for power outages or acts of God."

Langston shook his head. "I don't believe that would've gone over well with their parents who would've had to pay for the damages."

"My folks would have grounded me for life if that had happened."

"Speaking of your folks, how's your mother?"

Langston asking about Evelyn Powell was another reminder for Georgina to move out of her parents' house. "She's well."

What she wanted to tell him was that her mother had elevated manipulation to an art form. She'd feigned not feeling well whenever Georgina mentioned going out because Evelyn feared she would meet someone and possibly have a future with him.

"Tell her I asked about her."

"I will," she promised. Evelyn always perked up when someone asked about her. "How are your parents enjoying their retirement in Key West?"

"What can I say, Georgina. Dad just bought a boat that sleeps four. He, Mom and another couple sail down to different islands in the Caribbean to fish and shop, while using the boat as their hotel. I did ask them why they bought a bungalow when they spend most of their time on the water, and they couldn't give me an answer."

"Don't begrudge them, Langston. It sounds as if they're having the time of their lives."

He affected a half smile. "I suppose I'm a little jealous because they're having so much fun."

"Have you planned what you want to do once you retire?"

"No. I haven't thought that far ahead." He took a sip of champagne. "What about you, Georgi? Have you figured out your future?"

Langston shifted slightly to give her a direct stare, and Georgina sucked in an audible breath when she realized there was something in the way that he was looking at her, which made her feel slightly uncomfortable. Worldly and erudite, she wondered if he could see under the veneer of sophistication she'd affected for the fund-raiser to glimpse a girl in a woman's body struggling to control her destiny.

"Yes, but first I have to find someplace to live."

A frown appeared between his eyes. "Don't you live with your parents?"

When she'd met with Sasha Manning, her best friend from high school, to discuss her future, the pastry chef who'd recently opened Sasha's Sweet Shoppe on Main Street had advised her that in order to grasp a modicum of independence, she had to move out of her parents' house.

"Yes. I've made the decision to move out and get my own place."

"Where?"

"I'd prefer Wickham Falls, but if I can find something in Mineral Springs, I'll take it."

Langston gave her a *you've got to be kidding me* look when he said, "How can a girl who grew up in the Falls actually consider moving to the Springs? It just isn't done."

Georgina laughed, the sound carrying easily to a nearby table as several people turned to stare at her and Langston. The rivalry between the two towns had begun years ago during a high school football game when several players from Mineral Springs were charged with unnecessary roughness. The incident ended a player from the Falls the opportunity to take advantage of an athletic scholarship when his leg was so severely injured that he would never be able to compete again. Students from the Falls who dated people in the Springs were socially ostracized. It had become the modern-day version of the Hatfields and McCoys, with students in neighboring towns rather than families as archrivals.

"I know that, Langston, but I don't have a choice if I can't find something here in the Falls." Mineral Springs was larger, more populated, and there were several properties that were available for rent or purchase.

"Do you want to rent or buy?" he asked.

"It doesn't matter." Georgina had saved enough money for a sizable down payment on a house that would suit her tastes, but she was also willing to rent until she found a property where she hoped to spend the rest of her life. "You run a newspaper, so you must know just about everything that happens in Wickham Falls."

Langston affected a sly grin. "There are things I'm aware of and would rather not know. Have you checked with Viviana Remington? Correction. She's now Viviana Wainwright, and her husband is the developer who's building the new single-family homes on the Remington property. I would suggest you check with her before talking to a real-estate agent."

"Thanks for the tip. I'll let you know if I find something."

Georgina knew Viviana Remington was a direct descendant of the infamous Wolfe family who'd owned most of the coal mines in the county and were reviled for how they'd made their fortune taking advantage of their workers. And they preferred closing the mines rather than upgrade to meet the government's safety regulations. She was grateful to be seated at the table with Langston, because he'd given her the lead she needed to find somewhere to live before she sought out Miss Reilly, the local real estate agent.

He leaned close enough for their shoulders to touch. "I need a favor from you."

She went completely still. The last man who'd asked her for a favor needed fifteen thousand dollars to cover his gambling debts. He'd been siphoning money from the sale of cars at his father's used-car dealership to gamble, and when the accountant called to say he was coming to go over the books in order to file the corporate tax return, he panicked. Although they'd dated for almost eight months and Georgina thought she was in love with him, she ended their relationship and blocked his phone number.

She'd wanted to believe he was different because he worked for his father who had one of the most successful used-car dealerships in Beckley, but it was apparent he was no different from the men in the Falls who equated her to dollar signs. Boys in high school vied for her attention not because they'd thought her pretty, smart, or even talented, but because she was now sole heir to a business that had earned the reputation as the longest-running family-owned business in the town's history.

Georgina swallowed to relieve the constriction in her throat. "What do you want?"

Langston placed his hand over her fisted one. "Why do you make it sound as if I'm asking you to give up your firstborn?"

"That would be easy, because I don't have any children."

He angled his head. "Do you want children?"

His question gave her pause. It had been too many years since she had been involved with a man to even consider marriage and children. "I suppose I'd like one or two somewhere down the road."

Langston chuckled. "Just how long is that road, Georgi?"

She smiled. It was the second time he'd called her by the nickname kids in the Falls gave her to distinguish between her and another girl named Georgiana. "I really don't know, because I have a few requisites before I can even consider motherhood."

"Does finding a husband figure in your requisites?"

"That helps, but it's not mandatory."

"So," he drawled, "it wouldn't bother you to be an unwed mother?"

She scrunched up her nose. "I prefer the term *single mother*. If I decide to adopt a baby and not marry, I would be a single, not an unwed, mother."

Langston inclined his head. "Point taken."

"Now that we've settled that," she said after a pregnant pause, "what favor do you want from me?"

He leaned even closer, his nose brushing her ear. "Save a dance for me."

Georgina was shocked and relieved that all he wanted was a dance. The invitation indicated there would be music and dancing. "What if I save you two?"

Langston chuckled. "If I'd known you were that generous, then I would've asked for three or maybe even four."

"Don't push it, Langston."

He held up both hands. "Okay. Two it is."

Georgina didn't know Langston well, had had very little interaction with him in the past, yet she wanted to think of him as a friend. And she'd had very few close friends in the Falls other than Sasha Manning. She and Sasha had shared many of the same classes and confided in each other as to what they wanted once they graduated school. And now that Sasha had returned to town as a former contestant in a televised bakeoff, and the ex-wife of an A-list country singer, she'd sought her out to solicit her advice as to the steps she should take to realize her dream to become an independent businesswoman that did not include the department store.

Pushing back her chair, she rose to her feet, Langston rising with her. "Please excuse me, but Sasha just walked in and I need to talk to her."

Chapter Two

Langston watched Georgina walk, and felt as if he was able to breathe normally for the first time. He didn't know what it was about Georgina Powell that made him less confident in her presence than he was with other women he'd known or grown up with. The only other woman to have a similar effect on him he married. However, his ex-wife proved to be the opposite of Georgina, but he hadn't known that until after they were married. And, although he found it odd that as a thirty-something young woman Georgina still lived at home with her parents, he was curious to know the reason for her wanting to change residences.

He'd traveled the world, lived abroad for more

years than he could count and had interacted with people he wasn't certain were friend or foe. All of which served to hone and heighten his acuity when perceiving a situation. Langston did not want to relate to Georgina as a journalist, watching and waiting for a clue behind what she said, but as a man who'd found himself pleasantly enthralled with the very grown-up Georgina Powell.

She was at least three, or maybe even four, years his junior, which meant they did not share the same classes or friends, although they'd grown up in the same neighborhood. What they had in common was their parents were business owners. His parents, both pharmacists, owned the local pharmacy, and the Powells, the department store. By Wickham Falls' economic standards, the Coopers and Powells were considered well-to-do, but their social standing was of no import when they enrolled their children in the Johnson County Public School system. Every student was treated equally, which fostered an environment of one school, one team.

Langston was aware that despite its seemingly picture-postcard appearance with one- and two-story homes, and two traffic lights, and being touted as one of the best little towns in the state, Wickham Falls did have a history of labor unrest that came close to rivaling Matewan's coal-mining strikes, with months-long battles between union and nonunion workers. After the owners closed the mines, it taught the residents to depend on one another to ensure survival because of labor solidarity. And it was in the Falls that he felt more relaxed and able to recapture the peace he'd known and felt when growing up.

The decision to resign from the cable news station, where he'd worked as a foreign correspondent, sell his Washington, DC, condo and purchase the house in Wickham Falls from his parents after they'd retired and planned to live in their vacation home on Key West was an easy one for Langston. His contemplating buying a biweekly with a dwindling circulation was much more difficult. Despite becoming an award-winning journalist, and a *New York Times* bestselling nonfiction writer, he wasn't certain whether to invest in a newspaper when local papers had folded, and popular magazines were going from print to an electronic format.

He'd approached the owner of *The Sentinel* with an offer and after several weeks of negotiations, Langston had become the publisher and editor-in-chief of a failing paper. He'd thrown his experience and energies into revamping the biweekly's format, meeting several times a week with the staff to solicit their input for new ideas that would resurrect what had been a popular and necessary medium to disseminate information to the community. It had taken a year to realize an increase in circulation, and the paper's new design, columns and highlighting of individuals and businesses seemed to resonate with many subscribers.

Langston's focus shifted to Georgina as she laughed at something Sasha Manning said. He hadn't had any direct contact with her since returning. He'd caught glimpses of her whenever he went into the department store if she was summoned from the office to assist a customer or an employee. And he never would've suspected she had been hiding a magnificent figure under the loose-fitting smock and slacks. The generous slit in the body-hugging gown revealed a pair of slender, shapely legs and ankles in the sexy heels.

She's like Cinderella, he mused. During the day she went about with a bare face, shapeless clothes and her hair fashioned in a single braid; however, tonight she'd transformed into a seductress that had him and other men taking furtive glances at her.

Langston hadn't come back home to become involved with a woman; he'd come back to hopefully recover and heal from recurring episodes of PTSD, which had plagued him when he least expected. Spending too many years covering wars in two African countries and the Middle East had affected him psychologically. He'd gone into therapy to help cope with the nightmares, and it was only after he resigned his position as a correspondent had the macabre images decreased in frequency.

He stood up when Georgina returned to the table.

He pulled out her chair, seating her. Langston retook his seat and turned to look at the well-dressed elderly woman with bluish hair next to him when she rested a hand on his arm. Bessie Daniels had become a fixture in the town as the proprietress of Perfect Tresses hair salon. She'd begun using a blue rinse once she grayed prematurely and had earned the moniker of The Blue Lady.

"Langston, I wanted to tell you that I like what you've done with the newspaper. Eddie Miller ran *The Sentinel* into the ground after he took over from his father. What had been a fine newspaper was filled with reprinted articles no one cared about. Trust me, Langston, we don't mind reading about events that occurred a long time ago, but in my opinion, he was just too damn lazy to go out and gather current news to print."

"I'm glad you like the new format," he said. There was no way he was going to bash the former owner of the newspaper because not only did he still live in the Falls, but Bessie was an incurable gossip and whatever he said to her would no doubt be repeated and get back to Eddie.

"Your folks must be very proud of you, Langston."

He smiled. "I'd like to think they are."

"Please send them my best whenever you talk to or see them again."

"I will."

"By the way," Bessie continued, seemingly without taking a breath, "do you know why Bruce sent his daughter when he usually comes every year?"

Langston smothered a groan. He didn't know why the woman was interrogating him about something she probably knew, but just needed confirmation on. "I do not know." The four words were pregnant with a finality that he hoped she understood.

"Ladies and gentlemen, please be seated," came an announcement over the PA system. "Our mayor and the officers of the Chamber would like to say a few words before dinner is served."

"Nice timing," Georgina whispered in his ear.

Langston shared a knowing smile with her. It was apparent she'd overheard his conversation with Bessie Daniels. "Do you want to switch seats?" he teased, sotto voce.

"You're a big boy, Langston. Please don't tell me you're afraid of a harmless little lady."

He wanted to tell Georgina that the little lady was not harmless, and if the paper had a gossip column then he would've hired her. He'd added two new columns. "Sound Off", in which residents could anonymously voice their concerns about any or everything they felt strongly about, had replaced the "Letters to the Editor," and "Who's Who" to highlight residents who have made a difference. Langston blew out an audible breath when he realized Mrs. Daniels had turned her attention to the woman on her left. He had been given a pass from the chatty woman—for now.

* * *

The speakers droned on, and Georgina knew why her father had tired of attending the fund-raiser; there were too many speeches, which were much too long. She realized she had to get used to it because once she became a business owner it was incumbent she support the Chamber.

She lowered her head, hiding a smile when she saw Sasha roll her eyes upward while shaking her head. Her friend had turned heads in a chocolate-brown, off-the-shoulder dress with a revealing neckline. Georgina assumed it wasn't only the pastry chef's attire that had garnered attention, but also who she'd come with. Her date was the town's resident dentist and single father, Dr. Dwight Adams. Sasha had insisted her part-time employee's father was only a friend, and Georgina wondered, noticing the couple's entrancement with each other, how long they would remain friends. Even given the dearth of romance in her own life, Georgina was a romantic at heart, and she silently cheered for her friend to be given a second chance at love.

Now that she was focused on opening a craft shop, the notion of dating was not on her agenda and it nagged at her that she'd had to use subterfuge because she feared her father would use his influence to block her signing a lease on the vacant store around the corner from Main Street. Georgina had planned carefully when she directed an attorney to set up an LLC for her and gave them power of attorney to negotiate the terms of the lease on her behalf. With the executed lease, she'd applied to the town's housing department for a permit to operate a business and was currently awaiting their approval. The clerk at the town council told her there was a minimum two-month wait before her application would come up for review.

There had been a time when she resented her parents once they'd withdrawn their offer to pay the tuition for her to attend college because they expected her to assume complete control of Powell's once they retired. Georgina had argued they were nowhere near retirement age and her leaving home for four years would not negatively impact the viability of the store. As a recent high school graduate, she hadn't been aware of her mother's emotional instability. One moment she could be laughing, and then without warning she would dissolve into tears about losing her baby. Seeing her mother cry achieved the result Evelyn sought when Georgina promised she would stay. And she'd stayed for fourteen years while feeling as if she was losing a bit of herself day by day, hour by hour and minute by minute if she did not take control of her life and destiny.

Living with her parents and adhering to their rules had taken its toll on her own emotional well-being. She loved her mother and father, respected them as her parents, but she didn't want to turn into someone angry and resentful with the hand she'd been dealt because she had surrendered her will to others who had their own agenda.

"A penny for your thoughts, Georgi."

Langston's voice broke into her musings. "I can't believe how long these speeches are," she lied smoothly. Being deceitful did not come easily for Georgina, yet lately she'd become very closemouthed about her plans because she didn't want anything to come up that would delay or derail them.

"My folks told me when they first joined there wasn't a cocktail hour and the speeches went on for what appeared to be hours before dinner was served. That changed after some of the members threatened to leave the organization if the officers did not change the fund-raiser format."

"It's apparent they listened," she said, smiling.

"They didn't have a choice," Langston countered. "But there was a trade off. Membership dues and the price of the dinner tickets were increased to offset the cost of a cocktail hour. This year they've projected realizing a larger profit from the fund-raiser because they didn't have to rent space at the hotel because the Gibsons decided to donate this venue."

Georgina liked talking with Langston because he was a wealth of information about the goings-on in the town. The store had become her world, isolating her from everything outside the doors of Powell's Department Store.

She'd spend most of the day in the office, checking invoices, inventory, and managing payroll, while her father passed the time on the floor, interacting with customers and meeting with various vendors and deliverymen. And whenever she felt as if she was going stir-crazy, Georgina would leave the office to exchange pleasantries with customers, walk down to the bank to deposit receipts, or go across the street to Ruthie's for lunch. Working at the store since graduating high school had become a good and bad experience. Good because she'd learned the inner workings of to how to operate a business, and bad because after spending so many hours at the store she had little or no energy to do much more than take a long soak in the tub and go to bed, just to get up the next day and do it all over again.

She had already established hours for her own shop so she wouldn't work seven days a week, or ten hours a day, and it would be the first time when she would be able to balance work with possibly a future social life.

The speeches ended to rousing applause, and within minutes the waitstaff began serving those on the dais, town officials and then the assembly, while the DJ increased the volume on the music, but not so loud that one had to shout to be heard. Georgina had to admit her choice of roast capon with rosemary cider gravy, roasted cauliflower with scallion and lemon, and rice pilaf was not only appealing in presentation but also scrumptious. Meanwhile, bartenders wheeled carts around the room, filling beverage orders.

The man on her right, the owner of the laundromat/dry cleaner, talked incessantly about missing his wife of more than thirty years who'd died earlier in the year, and that running his business wasn't the same without her presence. The cheerful woman who'd manned the laundromat had greeted everyone with a smile, and most of the residents in the Falls turned out for her funeral.

Georgina had to admit, aside from the long-winded speeches, she was enjoying herself. Various floating conversations had her smiling when someone let it slip that a woman was cheating on her husband with their neighbor. She hadn't been to a social event since prom, so she did not have a frame of reference from which to ascertain whether the fund-raiser was an overwhelming success. The silent voice in her head chided her for not experiencing normal events a twenty- and thirty-something single woman would or should have. She'd become the good daughter in every sense of the word, but to her emotional detriment, which threatened to make her as socially reclusive as her mother.

She coveted what little free time she had occasionally watching her favorite TV shows, knitting or crocheting, and she had to thank her grandmother for teaching her the handicrafts passed down through

generations of Reed women. Grandmother Dorothea, or Dot, insisted she pay close attention when
she taught her to cast on stitches to knit her first
garment. Georgina proudly wore the scarf and then
began her next project—a crocheted ski cap. By the
time she'd celebrated her twelfth birthday she was
able to follow and complete difficult patterns uti-
lizing multiple colors, needles and hand or machine
quilting. Although Powell's had stocked fat quarters
for those who still pieced quilts, it had been years
since Georgina had made a quilt.

She had inherited a prized collection of antique
quilts hand sewn by her great-great-great-grand-
mother she had wrapped in tissue paper and stored
in moisture-free plastic containers on a top shelf of
her bedroom's walk-in closet.

Georgina shifted her attention to Langston.
"How's your fish?" He'd selected broiled flounder
stuffed with lump crab and topped with shrimp in
a béarnaise sauce.

"It's delicious. The Gibsons have outdone themselves tonight. I'm so used to their smoked brisket,
ribs and chicken that I had no idea they could get
hoity-toity on us."

Georgina laughed at Langston's description of
the dinner choices of roast prime rib with an herbed
horseradish crust, fish and chicken. "They had to
change it up if they want repeat business."

Langston draped his right arm over the back of her chair. "Do you ever go to the Den?"

"Hardly ever. Once I come home, I veg out."

"Are you saying it's all work and no play for you?" he asked.

"Just about. I work six days a week, and alternate Sundays with my father."

"That's a heavy schedule."

"It is. But I'm used to it." Georgina was used to it and she was counting down to the time when she would log a forty-hour workweek instead of an average of sixty-five. "How about you, Langston? Do you put in long hours?"

"It all depends. If I must cover a town council meeting in the evening, then I come in later in the day."

Georgina met his eyes, silently admiring the length of his lashes. It had been a while since she'd taken out her sketch pad to draw, but there was something about Langston's face that made her want to capture his image on paper. "Do you like working for yourself?" He smiled, bringing her gaze to linger on his mouth and still lower to the slight cleft in his strong chin.

"What I like is the flexibility. I have an incredible office manager who doesn't need me to be there to supervise her. She's been with the paper for years and she's not shy about telling me what our subscribers don't want. I trust her instincts because I've been away for almost twenty years."

Many young people left the Falls to go to college or enlist in the military, but Georgina had become the exception. "You left and I stayed." Georgina had spoken her musings aloud.

Langston leaned closer. "Did you ever think about leaving?"

Georgina lowered her eyes. "More times than I can count."

"What about now, Georgi?"

"I can't now."

"Are you engaged?"

A slow smile parted Georgina's lips. "No. I don't have time for a boyfriend. And if a man did ask me out, he'd have to have me home before midnight because I'm up at six and in the store at eight to get everything ready to open at nine."

"What about tonight? This event is scheduled to end sometime around one. Last year it wasn't over until after two."

"I'm not scheduled to work tomorrow." The store's Sunday hours were twelve noon to six.

"So Cinderella can stay out beyond midnight," Langston teased.

"She can stay out all night if she chooses."

Georgina could not remember the last time she'd stayed out all night. When she'd dated a man from Beckley, she would occasionally spend the night at his house even though she had to get up early the next morning to drive back to Wickham Falls. Her father knew she was sleeping with a man, but never broached the subject with her. After all, she was an adult and responsible for her own actions and behavior.

"Now if we were in DC or New York we could leave here and hang out at a jazz club and listen to music until the sun comes up. Then we would go to an all-night diner for breakfast."

She was intrigued by his supposition. "What would we do the next day?"

"Sleep in late. I'd also make dinner for you before taking you home."

Georgina laughed softly. "So you do cook."

A smile ruffled Langston's mouth. "I do all right."

"How much is all right?" she questioned.

"It depends on which type of cuisine you'd want. I'm partial to Middle Eastern and Mediterranean dishes."

Georgina slumped back in her chair, then sat straight when Langston's fingers grazed her exposed skin. His touch raised goose bumps on her arms as shivers eddied down her celibate body. And not for an instant could she forget that Langston Cooper was a very attractive man and eligible bachelor.

Langston had become a hometown celebrity after he was hired by a major all-news cable station where he was assigned to cover wars and skirmishes on the other side of the world. When his first book depicting his experience as a foreign correspondent was released it was as if every resident in Wickham Falls was reading it at the same time. The follow-up to his first book proved to be controversial when he was summoned to appear before a congressional committee where some members had accused him of being a spy or collaborating with enemy forces because of his knowledge of classified information. The charges proved unfounded. Langston resigned from the news station and returned home with superstar status.

"I'm really impressed," Georgina said after a noticeable pause. "I love Italian food."

"Do you have a preference?"

"Shrimp scampi and ravioli filled with any meat, cheese or vegetable."

"One of these days when you're free for dinner, I'll cook for you, always keeping in mind that you have to be home before midnight."

Georgina sobered quickly. She didn't want Langston to believe that she was flirting with him or soliciting a date. "You don't have to cook for me, Langston."

"Why are you sending me mixed messages?"

She went completely still. "Is that what I'm doing?"

"That's precisely what you're doing, Georgi. You tell me you love Italian food and when I offer to cook for you, you do a complete one-eighty. I can assure you that I don't have a dungeon in my home where I imprison unsuspecting young women in a modern-day Château d'If."

Georgina turned her head and bit her lip to keep from laughing in Langston's face. "Why are you being so melodramatic?"

"Is that what you believe? That I'm melodramatic?"

She shifted to face him again, putting her thumb and forefinger together. "Just a wee bit."

He smiled. "Maybe you're right. But I have to admit that you're the first woman since I've been back that I've invited to my home."

"Why me, Langston?" The instant the question rolled off her tongue Georgina chided herself for asking it. Why couldn't she just accept that he wanted to spend some time with her.

"Why not you, Georgi?"

Georgina did not have an answer for him. However, she couldn't help thinking he could be comparing her to the worldly, sophisticated women he'd met since leaving Wickham Falls, and found her gauche and gullible. Well, she was neither and she intended to prove it to him.

"I'll call you at your office to let you know when I'm available to come for dinner."

Reaching into the breast pocket of his jacket, he removed his cell phone and handed it to her. "Give me your cell number and I'll call you."

She wagged a finger. "Not yet. I'll give you my number but only after our first date." Langston's expression of surprise was priceless. It was apparent he wasn't used to women establishing the rules even before they had gone out together.

"Okay," he conceded. "I'll wait for your call. If I'm not in the office, then just leave a message with the receptionist."

Georgina felt as if she'd won a small victory, because she'd sworn after breaking up with her ex that she would never want another man to believe she was *that* grateful because he'd asked her out. She may not have had a lot of dates, but that did not make her feel diminished.

The tempo of the musician changed again, this time with more upbeat tunes as coffee and desserts were served. Several couples were already up on the dance floor, and minutes later others joined them. Pushing back his chair, Langston stood and offered Georgina his hand.

"May I please have this dance?"

She placed her hand on his outstretched palm, smiling as he eased her to stand. The music selection was a slow, romantic tune. He led her to the dance floor, and her body molded against his when his arm curved around her waist. Georgina closed her eyes as she lost herself in the smell of his cologne, the warmth of his breath in her ear and his protective embrace that allowed her to temporarily forget why

she'd refused to date a man from her hometown. And
if she did share dinner with Langston in his home, he
would become the first. However, unlike other men
from Wickham Falls, she wasn't concerned that his
interest in her was wholly financial. Not only was
he a business owner, but he was also a bestselling
writer. Georgina wasn't looking for a boyfriend, or
even a committed relationship, and for her, cultivat-
ing a friendship with the editor-in-chief of the local
newspaper would be a plus.

The song ended and she kissed Langston's jaw.
"Thank you for the dance and I owe you another
one, but I have to leave because I just remembered
I have to meet someone early tomorrow morning."

Nodding, Langston escorted her back to their
table, waited for her to retrieve her shawl and evening bag, and then walked her out to the parking lot.
"Get home safely."

She gave him a warm smile. "Thank you. And
you get home safely yourself." Georgina started up
her vehicle and maneuvered out of the crowded lot.
Although she wasn't scheduled to work the next day,
she needed to get up in time to drive to the town's
only bed-and-breakfast to confer with Noah Wainwright about his construction project. The sooner she
initiated her plan to move, the sooner she would be
able to tackle the next item on her journey to achieve
independence.

Chapter Three

Georgina walked into the kitchen early Sunday morning to find her parents sitting in the breakfast nook. "You guys are up early."

"So are you," Evelyn countered. "I thought you would've slept in this morning."

She picked up a mug and popped a coffee pod into the single-serve coffeemaker. "I would've if I didn't have to meet someone."

"Does your someone have a name?"

Georgina stared at her mother. Evelyn Reed Powell had lost at least twenty pounds following her son's death and had never regained it, leaving her to appear emaciated. Her dark brown complexion appeared unhealthy, while her once-thick black hair was now sparse, graying wisps. The extremely attractive woman who had become the envy of most young women in the Falls when she got Bruce Powell to not only profess his love for her but also claim her as his wife. Once she became aware of her mother's depression, Georgina begged her to seek treatment, but Evelyn refused, declaring there was nothing wrong with her.

Bruce frowned at his wife. "Let it go, Evelyn. Have you forgotten Georgina is a grown woman and entitled to her own privacy?"

Evelyn rounded on him. "As long as she lives under my roof, I have a right to know where she's going and who she's seeing."

The fragile rein Georgina had on her temper when interacting with her mother snapped. "That's not going to be much longer," she spat out. She hadn't planned to inform her parents she was moving until she found a place to live.

Evelyn looked as if she was going to faint. "What!"

Georgina pressed the button on the coffeemaker harder than necessary. "I said I'm moving out."

"What about the store?" Bruce questioned.

She smiled at her easygoing father. He'd lost most of his bright red hair and now at fifty-nine was left with a fringe on the crown of his head. There were times when she wondered how he had put up with his controlling wife, but it was apparent he was either used to or ignored most of her complaints.

"I'll still be working in the store."

Georgina didn't have the heart to tell him that she wasn't certain how long that would be. She'd contacted her first cousin, Sutton Reed, who had not renewed his contract with a Major League Baseball team after he'd suffered a season-ending injury. He had promised to let her know when he would return to Wickham Falls to help his uncle manage the store for a year while he contemplated life after baseball. Other than Sasha, only Sutton knew she wanted to leave the department store to go into business for herself.

Bruce exhaled an audible breath. "That's good to know."

"But she can't leave!" Evelyn screamed.

"Yes, she can, Evelyn. Have you forgotten that our daughter is thirty-two years old and she should've lived on her own years ago? It's you who doesn't want her to leave."

"I lost my son and now I can't bear to lose my daughter."

Georgina rolled her eyes upward as she ignored her mother's forced tears. "You're not losing me, Mom. I'm moving out, not away."

"I'm still losing you."

She'd had enough of the theatrics. Georgina poured the coffee into a travel mug, added a splash of cream, secured the top and walked out of the kitchen. She wasn't about to get into an argument with her mother because there would be no winners, only losers. And while she'd always bitten her tongue or walked away before she said something that would completely fracture her relationship with the older woman, Georgina knew she was through being diplomatic. Come hell or high water, she was moving.

Georgina parked her car in the space designated for guest parking at the antebellum-designed B and B. It was the largest and most impressive house in the town and had been known as the Wolfe House, the Falls House and now currently the Wickham Falls Bed-and-Breakfast.

Her contact with Viviana and her brother Leland was nearly nonexistent when growing up because they'd attended a private boarding school. When Viviana married New York City-based developer and real-estate mogul, Noah Wainwright, some of the locals were grumbling that money begat money. There were three other cars in the lot beside hers, and she hoped Noah would be available to talk to her.

After walking up the front steps to the mansion, Georgina opened the front door as a chime signaled someone had come in. Viviana appeared as if out of nowhere, and Georgina smiled at the tall, slender woman with a wealth of black, curly hair framing her face and cascading down her back.

She extended her hand. "I'm Georgina and—"

"I know who you are," Viviana said, cutting her off and taking the proffered hand. "Even though we live in the same town I rarely get a chance to leave this place. Is there something I can help you with?"

Viviana was right, because she'd had very little interaction with the woman who'd occasionally come into the store to buy yarn or fabric. She noticed the circle of diamonds in the eternity band on Viviana's left hand. "First, congratulations on your marriage."

Clear, toffee-brown eyes in a flawless golden-brown complexion crinkled when she smiled. "Thank you. I'm still attempting to get used to introducing myself as Wainwright rather than Remington."

"I'm certain a lot of newlywed brides have the same problem," Georgina said.

"Even though all of the guests haven't come down for breakfast I could get the cook to fix you a plate."

"Please, no. I came to ask your husband about the homes that are being built on your land."

"Noah's in New York, but maybe I can help you. Come into my office so we can talk in private."

Georgina followed Viviana through the grand entryway to a room where the proprietress had set up her office. "This place is magnificent."

Viviana waited for her to sit before taking a

matching needlepoint chair opposite her. "You wouldn't have said that if you'd been here almost two years ago. Thanks to my brother, I was able to make repairs and restore the furnishings to where they are almost new. This place was a boardinghouse before I converted it to a B and B. Half the bedroom suites are set aside for the business and the other half for personal living. I know I've been running off at the mouth when you want to know about the houses that are under construction."

"Yes. I'd like to know if any are completed and up for sale."

"Only the model homes are completed. It will be at least another six to eight months before the rest of the structures will be ready for sale and occupancy."

Georgina schooled her expression not to show her disappointment. "I'm planning to move out of my parents' home, and I was looking for something here in the Falls either to buy or rent until I decide on something permanent."

"I have two vacant fully furnished guesthouses on the property you can rent."

How much Viviana was going to charge her to rent the guesthouse wasn't a deal breaker because Georgina preferred living in the Falls. And the last time she went through the classified ads in *The Sentinel* there was one house for sale and listed as a fixer-upper. She had no intention of investing her money in a property that needed extensive repairs even before she could move in.

"Is this a good time for you to show them to me?"

Viviana smiled. "It's perfect."

When Viviana tapped the key card and opened the door, Georgina couldn't stop grinning. Her eyes lit up like a child's on Christmas morning when seeing piles of gaily wrapped gifts under the decorated tree. The guesthouses were far enough away from each other and the main house to ensure complete privacy, and the interior claimed two bedrooms with sitting areas, flat-screen TVs, and there was a loft with a king-size bed overlooking the living/dining area. It also had a galley kitchen and full bathroom with a freestanding shower. A stackable washer/dryer unit was concealed in a closet off the bathroom.

The furniture was contemporary, upholstered in red, brown and green, and was a colorful contrast to the lemon-yellow walls. A desk, worktable and chair positioned in a corner under a window was the perfect spot for her to set up a computer program for her business. She could use the extra bedroom to store her inventory rather than continue to pay a storage company. A wall of French doors spanned the rear of the house, allowing for unlimited light during the day.

"As a guest you're entitled to a buffet breakfast from seven to ten. Cordials and desserts are served in the parlor at 8:00 pm, and the entire property is wired with cable and Wi-Fi. You're entitled to daily housekeeping services, and if you need clean linen then leave the placard on the bed."

"It's perfect for my needs," Georgina told Viviana. "Is it possible for me to rent it until the houses are completed?"

"Yes. The rental rates vary for month-to-month, or three, six, nine and twelve months. If you decide to rent for six months, then you will get a twenty percent discount than if you decide for three."

She thought about the projected two-month minimum wait for the approval of the permit to open her shop. "What if I rent the guesthouse for three months with an option for an additional three?"

A pregnant silence ensued as Viviana appeared to be deep in thought. "If that's the case then I'll charge you the six-month rate, which should allow you a greater discount. And if you move out before six months, then I'll prorate the difference. I can't have folks who live in the Falls talk about me cheating them. Even though Leland and I are Remingtons, people seem to get a kick out of reminding us that our mama was a Wolfe and Daddy was a junkie."

Georgina had grown up eavesdropping on conversations between her mother and other women whispering about Emory Remington. His military career ended when he was wounded during a deployment, and his dependence on prescribed meds segued into addiction to heroin and subsequent imprisonment for armed robbery to get money to support his habit. And anyone claiming Wolfe blood was reviled because of their corrupt, immoral ancestors.

"And the same hypocrites have so many skeletons in their closets that if you open them, they would rattle like dice."

"I agree with you," Viviana said. "It's always the ones with the most to hide who are always beating their gums about something. Let's go back to the house and I'll review the rates with you."

An hour after Georgina walked into the B and B, she left with a rental agreement and a key card for her new residence. The moment she handed Viviana her credit card she realized although she'd lived in Wickham Falls all her life, it was if she was starting over.

Renting a fully furnished house was convenient, because she didn't have to buy furniture or kitchen items. All she had to do was pack her clothes and personal items and shop for groceries to stock the fridge and pantry. Although she could take advantage of the B and B's buffet breakfast, Georgina planned to prepare her own meals.

Her father's car wasn't in the driveway, which meant he was probably at the store. She went into the house and found her mother in the family room watching her favorite televangelist. The Sundays she was off, Georgina had invited Evelyn to attend church services with her, but when her mother appeared to be mute, she'd stopped asking. Georgina knew it wasn't healthy for her mother to stay indoors for weeks on end and had stopped attempting to devise scenarios to get Evelyn to leave the house.

"Mom, did you eat breakfast?"

Evelyn glanced at her. "I had toast and coffee."

"I'm making an omelet. Do you want one?"

"No, thank you."

"What about fruit? There's still some cantaloupe and honeydew left."

"I'll have fruit."

Georgina found it hard to believe Evelyn had agreed to eat more than her usual toast and coffee. Perhaps announcing that she was moving out had penetrated her mother's shroud of self-pity, and awakened the reality that she could no longer depend on her daughter for companionship when she had a husband who loved her unconditionally.

"Do you want to eat in the family room or in the kitchen with me?"

"As soon as my show is over, I'll join you in the kitchen."

She went into the kitchen to make her Sunday breakfast favorite—an omelet, fresh fruit and wheat toast. Sundays she didn't work, she usually cooked different meats and side dishes to last for several days. Georgina had defrosted pork chops, a couple of pounds of large shrimp and a roasting chicken.

She'd also planned to make a black bean soup with andouille sausage, baked macaroni and cheese, corn muffins and cranberry bread pudding with bourbon custard and cranberry sauce.

Whenever she cooked, Georgina felt as if she was paying homage to her Grandma Dot. Growing up, she'd believed there wasn't anything her grandmother did not do well. She was an incredible cook and was disappointed that her daughters were less than enthusiastic about following in her footsteps. However, Dot's faith was restored when her only granddaughter inherited her love of cooking and needlework. And once Georgina exhibited a talent for drawing it was Grandma Dot who'd encouraged her to become an artist. She missed her grandmother but knew she would be proud of her once she opened the shop that she planned to call A Stitch at a Time.

Georgina had just finished chopping the ingredients for the omelets when she noticed Evelyn standing at the entrance to the kitchen. "Please come in, Mom, and sit down."

"So you're really serious about moving out?" Evelyn asked as she entered the kitchen and sat on a stool at the cooking island.

"Yes."

"When?"

"Sometime this week. I'll start loading up my car in a few days to begin moving my clothes and other personal items."

Closing the storage unit and storing the boxes in the smaller of the two bedrooms in the guesthouse had become Georgina's priority. And although she had to wait for the town's building department to approve the permit for her to open the craft shop, she felt confident it would become a reality. The landlord had renovated the space and added a bathroom after the last tenant vacated, brought everything up to code, and it was now turnkey ready.

She had also ordered shelving, reception-area furniture and chairs and loveseats for an area she'd planned to set aside for her customers to relax while working on their handmade projects. There would also be a refreshment station with water, coffee, tea and baked goods from Sasha's Sweet Shoppe.

"You've found a place." Evelyn's query was a statement.

"Yes, Mom. I'm renting one of the guesthouses on the Remington property."

"Do you really want to get involved with *those* people?"

Georgina glared at her mother. "When are you going to let it go that Viviana and her brother aren't responsible for how the Wolfes treated folks who worked in their mines?"

"Never," Evelyn said, frowning. "The Wolfes fired my grandfather after he was diagnosed with black lung disease. They claimed it had come from his smoking cigarettes, and I still remember his having to drag around an oxygen canister to help him breathe. He died cursing the Wolfes once they'd begun closing the mines one by one because the bastards didn't want to comply with the government's safety regulations."

"Mom, you have to forgive what happened over which you had no control, even if you choose not to forget."

"Like that boy who tried to extort you for money to pay his gambling debts?"

Georgina regretted telling her mother why she'd stopped dating Sean Bostic despite promising him she wouldn't tell anyone, yet she hadn't wanted to lie about why she'd abruptly ended their eight-month relationship. Instead of being supportive that a man had attempted to take advantage of her daughter, Evelyn appeared to celebrate the breakup because it meant Georgina wasn't going to get married and leave her.

"There's nothing to forgive because I didn't give Sean any money. But I did learn a lesson about not ignoring the signs whenever a man talks about money, whether it's his or mine."

"You have to know that a lot of men these days are looking for a woman to take care of them. A prime example is my sister Michelle. Once Sutton's father discovered she'd inherited some money from our Daddy's life insurance he latched on to her like a leech, while sweet-talking her into buying him a new car and whatever else he wanted. And, when the money ran out, he also ran out, leaving her practically barefoot and pregnant."

Georgina remembered her aunt Michelle cackling like a hen laying an egg when she'd revealed to her sister that Sutton's father came skulking back like a whipped dog after the news that his son, whom he'd never met, after graduating college had become a first-round draft pick for a major league baseball team. The first-base, homerun-hitting phenom who'd signed a multimillion-dollar, four-year contract wanted nothing to do with the man who'd deserted his mother when she'd needed him most.

"Aunt Michelle may have had to raise her son as a single mother, but in the end, she came out the winner and her baby daddy the loser. What was one of Grandma Dot's favorite sayings?"

Evelyn's eyebrows lifted questioningly. "Which one? She had so many that I couldn't keep track of them. Like 'what doesn't come out in the wash will come out in the rinse.' Or 'she took the rag off the bush.'"

"It's the one about getting by but not getting away. In other words, karma is always waiting at the end of the road before she decides to punch your expiration ticket."

Evelyn flashed a rare smile. "I've lived long enough to see folks reap what they've sown, and most times it's not a good deed."

"You're only fifty-nine, so you're not that old."

"There are times when I feel so much older," Evelyn admitted.

"That's because you spend so much time alone in the house. You should ask Dad to take some time off and go somewhere exotic where the most strenuous thing you'd have to do is raise your hand to get the attention of the resort employee to bring you something to eat or drink."

"I can't do that."

"And why not, Mom?"

"What about the store?"

Georgina narrowed her eyes at her mother at the same time she pressed her lips together to stop the acerbic words from coming out. Evelyn was the queen of excuses. And if she said it, then she tended to believe it. "Do you really think the store is going to close its doors if Dad isn't there for a week? Remember when he came down with the flu a couple of years ago, and I took care of everything? Powell's may not be as large as other department stores, but we've been in business for more than one hundred years, and chances are it will continue long after we're gone."

"You know there's an unwritten rule that the store has to be managed by a family member, so what's going to happen if you don't get married and have children?"

"I don't have to be married to have children,

Mom. I could always adopt. And don't forget I'm not the only Powell. Dad still has a brother and sister who both have kids."

"Paul just retired from the army after twenty-five years, and there's no way he's going to give up living in Hawaii to come back to the Falls. And forget about Donna. She's never going to leave Alaska, her husband, children, grandchildren and her beloved sled dogs."

"Not to worry, Mom. Dad's not ready to retire, so that's something we don't have to think about until years from now."

Georgina talking to Evelyn while she cooked felt like old times before Kevin passed away. She wasn't certain whether her mother had accepted what she couldn't change—her moving out or realizing that her inability to solicit her husband as an ally was futile.

"Maybe I'll ask your father if he would like to take a few days off and go away."

"Do you have an idea of where you would like to go?"

"Definitely someplace warm. Maybe we can go to Hawaii to visit Paul."

Georgina flashed a smug grin. Getting her parents to go away for a week or two would be good for both of them. She'd proven in the past that she could manage the store without her father's presence, and during their absence she would stay at the house.

"Make certain to take a lot of pictures."

"Your father can do that. I can't take a decent picture if my life depended on it. Speaking of pictures, did you take any at the fund-raiser?"

"No, but Jonas Harper was there representing the town and the newspaper. I'm certain there will be a lot of pictures in the next issue."

"Was Langston there to cover it for the paper?"

"Yes. In fact, we shared a table."

"It's a shame his wife cheated on him with that so-called actor while he'd risked life and limb covering wars on the other side of the world."

Georgina did not understand how her mother was privy to so much gossip when she hardly ventured outside the house. Did she keep in touch with someone who kept her abreast of the goings-on in town, or had she pumped her husband for information and then drew her own conclusions?

She set the table in the breakfast nook with bowls of sliced melon and quickly made two Western omelets. Evelyn devoured it, saying it was delicious, and Georgina didn't want to declare an early victory in getting her mother to eat, but it was a start.

Evelyn retreated to the family room to watch television, while Georgina cleaned up the kitchen before taking out the ingredients she needed to prepare Sunday dinner.

It was Monday morning and minutes before seven when Georgina pulled into her reserved parking space behind the department store an hour before her normal arrival time. Most of the businesses along Main Street were still closed; the lights coming from the popular restaurant Ruthie's indicated they were preparing for their all-you-can-eat buffet. She noticed a car from the sheriff's department parked at the far end of the lot. Since being elected and sworn in as sheriff, Seth Collier had increased patrols of the downtown business district after an attempted break-in at the pharmacy. He'd suspected the burglar or burglars were looking for drugs. Residents of Wickham Falls were not exempt from the opioid epidemic sweeping the country.

She unlocked the rear door, disarmed the security system and then closed and locked it behind her. Before her father closed at night, he had made it a practice to leave a few lights on so if the sheriff or his deputies checked stores in the downtown business district, they were able to view the interiors to detect possible intruders.

She punched in the code to the office and walked in. Last year the space had undergone a complete renovation with a new coat of paint, ceiling tiles, carpeting and recessed lighting. A glazer had installed one-way windows, which allowed her to observe all activity on the sales floor. Security cameras were installed throughout the building to deter shoplifting. Her father had also updated the employees' break room and bathrooms.

After placing a container with her lunch from the dishes she'd prepared the day before in the office's mini fridge, she picked up the telephone and dialed the number to *The Sentinel*, listening for the prompts on the voice mail messaging. It wasn't the recorded message that greeted her, but a familiar male's voice.

"Langston?"

"All day and all night."

Georgina smiled. She hadn't expected Langston to answer the phone at this hour in the morning. "Good morning, Langston. Do you usually begin working this early?"

"No. The office doesn't open until nine. I'm here because I didn't go home last night."

"You spent the night there?"

"Yes. I began writing a piece on the Chamber fund-raiser and lost track of time. I should finish it in a couple of hours, then I'll go home and crash."

"I'm not going to keep you. I just called to thank you for recommending the Wainwrights, because I'll be renting one of their guesthouses. The new homes are still under construction, and probably won't be ready for sale until the end of the year."

"I'm glad you found something in Wickham Falls."

"Me, too," Georgina said in agreement. She was more than glad and had to tamp down feelings of euphoria whenever she thought about moving into the guesthouse.

"Once you're settled in, we have to get together so I can make my butternut squash ravioli for you."

She smiled again. "Okay. I'll call and let you know when I can come up for air."

"Take down my cell number. If you can't reach me here, then you can always send me a text."

Reaching for a pen, Georgina wrote down the ten digits, and then repeated it to Langston. "I'm going to give you my number, so you won't have to call me here at the store."

A low chuckle caressed her ear. "What's so funny?"

"You, Georgi. First you claim you won't give me your number until after we have our first date, and now you've reneged."

"Have you ever changed your mind about something?"

"Yeah."

"There you go. Now, take down my number before I change my mind again."

"Talk to me, Cinderella."

She gave him the number to her cell phone. "If I'm Cinderella, then who are you?"

A beat passed. "I haven't yet decided whether I'm the prince from *Sleeping Beauty* or *Cinderella*."

"You can't mix fairy-tale princes, Langston. And, how do you know so much about princes and princesses?"

"My mother used to read them over and over to my sister."

"By the way, how is your sister doing?"

"Jackie's well. She's left teaching for a while to become a stay-at-home mom and she loves it."

Jacklyn Cooper, who'd been in Georgina's graduating class, left the Falls to enroll in Howard University as an English major. "Give her my regards when you talk to her. I'm going to hang up now so you can finish your article, go home and get some sleep."

"Okay. Later."

"Later, Langston."

Georgina ended the call and then leaned back in the desk chair. Langston said inviting her to his house for dinner was a date. And he'd also revealed that she would be the first woman he would invite to his home since his return. He'd been back a little more than a year and she wondered why her and not some other woman.

Cinderella. Had he likened her to the fairy-tale princess because she'd informed him that she had to be home before midnight; or did he view her as the young woman who hadn't been permitted to leave home until she met her prince who'd freed her from a life of monotony? And, she mused, did she need rescuing? Or did she want Langston to become her prince?

If she was truthful, then she would have to give Sasha Manning credit for hearing her out and suggesting she move out of her parents' home for the first step in establishing her independence. Sasha had left the Falls within months of graduation, while Georgina had given up her dream of leaving and attending art school. Whenever she heard that another of her classmates had gone to college, enlisted in the military, or even accepted employment outside Johnson County, she sank further into a morass of helplessness until she'd accepted her plight. She would live at home and work for the family-owned business.

Once her father began downsizing the arts and craft section the lightbulb in her head was suddenly illuminated. Bruce claimed he wanted to expand the sporting goods area and had contacted the vendor selling yarn and fabric to cancel all future orders. She'd stayed after hours to box up the entire craft materials section and took it to a storage company in Mineral Springs. Yards of yarn and bolts of fabric had become her one-way ticket to a life she never would've imagined if her father hadn't decided to scale back the inventory.

Smiling, Georgina booted up the store's computer and clicked on the app for accounts payable. She'd computerized all vendors, paid them electronically and direct-deposited payroll checks into employees' bank accounts. Her father oversaw the front of the store and monitored the clerks checking out customers and would periodically empty the registers of cash and store it in the office safe.

Powell's had had two burglaries in the past, and an armed robbery several years ago. Unfortunately for the perpetrator, he was unaware that a plain-clothes deputy on loan from Mineral Springs was at checkout and managed to disarm and apprehend him before he could escape. The incident prompted her father to install panic buttons under the counters at checkout, which were wired directly to the sheriff's office.

The office door opened, and Bruce walked in. "I can't believe you got here before me."

Georgina smiled at her father. He'd shaved his head. She'd suggested he get rid of the circle of fading red hair a long time ago like so many men who were balding. "How handsome you look."

Attractive lines fanned out around Bruce's dark-blue eyes when he smiled. "I know you've been after me to shave my head, and I must admit it's really liberating. I'm certain Joe's Barber is going to miss me, but I'll still go there for a professional shave every couple of weeks. Now, why did you get up before the chickens?"

"I want to get most of my paperwork done so I can leave a little early to go home and start packing."

Bruce sat on a chair next to the workstation. "I'm glad you decided to move out."

"What!"

"I'd wanted to tell you a long time ago that you should live on your own. But I didn't want to start up with your mother. Speaking of your mother," he continued without taking a breath, "she suggested we go to Hawaii to visit Paul and his family."

Georgina studied her father's face, realizing for the first time that she was a softer, more feminine version of the man. Whenever he came to her school, kids would announce loudly that her father was there to see her. Grandma Dot used to say that Bruce Powell had figuratively spit her out.

"Are you going?"

"I'm seriously thinking about it. When I called Paul, he said he was looking forward to having us come. But if I do go, then you're going to have to spend most of your time on the floor."

"Don't worry, Dad. I'll ask Dan Jackson if he's willing to work security until you get back." Dan had become a lifer in the corps, and after separating worked security for private social events.

Bruce's pale eyebrow lifted. "I guess that settles it. You call Dan while I research flights."

"How long do you plan to stay?"

"Probably a week to ten days." He placed his hand over Georgina's and gave her fingers a gentle squeeze. "Thank you, baby girl."

A slight frown creased her forehead. "For what, Dad?"

"I believe you telling your mother you were moving out made her aware that she didn't have to depend on you for companionship. I told her she would never be alone if I'm alive, because I'd made a vow to be with her through the good times and the bad ones. I love her just that much."

"Why did it take her this long to come to the realization that she does have a loving and supportive husband?" Georgina asked.

"I'm not complaining about how long it took, because I've been given a second chance to get my wife back."

Georgina did not want to ask, but she wondered if her mother had even spurned her husband's attempt to make love to her. "You can think of it as a second honeymoon."

Bruce smiled. "That's what I'm hoping."

"If Mom comes back pregnant, I'm going to disown both of you," she teased.

He jerked back his hand as if hers had burned him as blood drained from his face, leaving it a sickly yellowish shade. "Your mama had a difficult delivery with Kevin, and the doctor couldn't stop the bleeding, and subsequently she had a hysterectomy that made it impossible for her to have another child. That's part of the reason she was so devastated when he died."

Georgina covered her mouth with her hand and closed her eyes. She had no idea that her mother had undergone a hysterectomy. She'd believed Evelyn had spent a lot of time in bed because she'd had a Cesarean.

"I'm sorry, Daddy. Why didn't you tell me?"

Bruce's expression softened. "Your mother made me swear never to tell anyone. Are you aware that it's been years since you've called me *Daddy*?"

Rising slightly, she leaned over and kissed his smooth-shaven jaw. "Is that what you want me to call you?"

Bruce ran a hand over her curly hair. "No. I'm waiting for the day when you'll call me Grandpa."

Georgina hadn't missed the longing tone in her father's voice. "Give me time to get my life together, and one of these days I'll hope to make you a grandfather."

"Don't wait too long, sweetie, or I'll be too old to toss my grandbaby in the air and catch them."

She cut her eyes at her father. "You will not toss my babies."

"Have one or two, then we'll see." Bruce stood up. "It's time I get the register drawers."

Georgina focused her attention on the computer screen while Bruce opened the safe and removed the drawers to the registers. He'd made it a practice to fill them the night before, which eliminated the need to count out bills and coins before the clerks arrived.

The weekend had been full of surprises. She'd attended a social affair and was seated with a man who'd invited her to his home for a dinner date; she'd revealed to her parents that she was moving out; had rented a house that would fulfill her current needs;

her father and mother were going on vacation for the first time in years, and he'd revealed the underlying cause for his wife's depression.

Georgina was annoyed with her father because if he'd told her about Evelyn's inability to have more children, she wouldn't have spent so many years resenting her mother's need to cling to her surviving child because she feared losing her, too. She also faulted him because he should've tried harder to help his wife deal with her grief and not sanction her emotional manipulation of their daughter.

Her father wanted grandchildren, but that could not become a reality until Georgina was able to cross off several more items on her wish list.

Chapter Four

Langston studied the gallery of photographs that were taken two weeks ago at the Chamber dinner on the computer monitor. While Jonas Harper was Wickham Falls' official photographer, he also freelanced for the paper. The man truly was an artistic genius. He'd photographed every table, and his lens had captured expressions ranging from stoic to ebullient.

A smile tilted the corners of his mouth. The lens had captured an image of him and Georgina smiling at each other as if sharing a secret. When he'd left the Falls to attend college, Georgi was a cute teenage girl. Fast-forward more than a decade and she was now a stunning woman.

Her sensual voice, the way in which she glanced up at him through her lashes, and her fluid body language were traits that had him thinking about her days later. And he hadn't lied when he revealed she would become the first woman he'd invited to his home. The house where he'd grown up had become his sanctuary, a place filled with warm and happy memories of his childhood.

His parents were protective, and affectionate with one hard and fast rule that he and his sister do well in school because without an education he would never be able to realize his dream to become a journalist. Langston struggled to balance sports with academics when he joined the baseball team as a pitcher, and during his junior year when his grades began to slip he had to decide which he craved more—the roar of the crowd when he struck out someone on the opposing team, or getting into the college of his choice. In the end it was the latter.

His private line rang, and he tapped the speaker feature when he saw the name on the console. "I got them, Jonas."

"What do you think, Lang?"

"They're incredible. Your lens is pure magic."

Jonas laughed. "I had to use a long lens so not to be obtrusive. Folks tend not to be so candid when you put a camera in their face. You look really cozy with Powell's daughter."

"We had fun."

"No doubt. Did you find the one where you were dancing together?"

"Not yet."

"Keep scrolling and you'll see what I'm talking about. You told me you wanted to include a two-page spread in the upcoming edition, so if you want me to include it you should be ready when folks talk about you hooking up with Powell's girl."

"She happens to have a name, Jonas."

"I know, but everyone refers to her as Powell's girl."

Langston scrolled through the photos until he came to the one with him dancing with Georgina. She'd closed her eyes, her head resting on his shoulder. And his expression said it all. He was enjoying having her in his arms.

"Let them talk, Jonas." He'd witnessed too much death and dying up close and personal to concern himself with gossip. He'd survived being embedded with troops in war zones and had been absolved of being a spy and/or traitor after the publication of his second book by a congressional committee, so chitchat or innuendos were inconsequential to his well-being.

"I hear you, man. I've numbered each of the captions to correspond with the photos and I'm now uploading them to you."

"Thanks, Jonas. Don't forget to send me an invoice so I can pay you."

"You bet."

Langston ended the call, propped his feet on the edge of the desk and stared at the rain sluicing down the windows. The temperatures hinting of an early spring had dropped drastically and it felt more like December than early April.

A light tapping on the door garnered his attention, and lowering his feet, he swiveled in the executive chair to see the middle-aged man who was responsible for advertising. Within days of purchasing the paper, Langston called a staff meeting and advised everyone their position was at risk if the circulation and the number of ads continued to decrease. Randall Stone had become the focus of the meeting because he headed advertising.

"Yes, Randall?

"When do you plan to send the paper to the printer?"

Langston stared at the pale, slender man who'd relocated to London to live with a widow he'd met on the internet. He spent eight years there before deciding that he missed the States *and* Wickham Falls. He returned home, married a divorcée with two adult sons and claimed he was living his best life.

"I'd like to deliver it Wednesday. Why?" If he didn't get the issue to the printer before midnight on Thursdays, then it would be too late to print the paper.

"I'm still waiting for Powell's Easter sale ad. Do you want me to go there in person to pick it up?"

"No, Randall. I'll contact Bruce to find out about the delay." The owner of the department store usually took out a full-page ad for most major holidays.

Randall affected a snappy salute. "Okay."

Langston waited until he was alone to buzz the receptionist. "I'll be out for a while. Please take my messages."

Pulling on a rain poncho he covered his head with a baseball cap and headed for the back staircase to the street level. He didn't mind the cold, heat, or even snow. But there was something about getting drenched that annoyed him. His mother used to tease him saying he was part feline.

He sprinted down the street to Powell's and waited for the automatic doors to open. Other than Ruthie's, the department store was Langston's favorite place to shop. It was stocked with countless items including housewares, party goods, CDs and DVDs, candy, sporting goods, cleaning, beauty and school supplies. Many of the discs in his permanent music and movie collection he'd purchased from Powell's. There weren't many customers in the store, and he attributed that to the weather.

Langston approached a clerk near the checkout counter. "Is Mr. Powell around?"

"No, sir. Mr. Powell is on vacation. His daughter is in the office. Do you want me to page her?"

"Please."

He exchanged a nod of recognition with Dan Jackson as the man slowly walked up and down aisles. The highly trained ex-military sniper had begun a second career when he opened a security and protection business, only hiring former military.

Langston could not stop staring when he saw Georgina make her way to the front of the store. It wasn't the first time he'd observed her not wearing makeup; however, he was shocked to see the bluish circles under her clear brown eyes that made it impossible for him to look away. Even her face was thinner, and she looked as if she hadn't slept in days. He wondered if she wasn't feeling well.

"Are you all right?"

"What happened to good afternoon, Georgi?"

Langston clamped his jaw tightly. She wanted to engage in pleasantries when he wanted answers. He knew he had no right to be concerned about her physical well-being, yet he was. Talking and dancing with Georgina at the fund-raiser was a blatant reminder of what he'd been missing even before his marriage ended. It had taken a while for him to forgive his ex-wife for her duplicity but he eventually realized he'd contributed to her seeking companionship with another man. He'd known of her unresolved childhood issues surrounding abandonment, when they were separated for months, and there were times when she hadn't known whether he was dead or alive.

"Good afternoon," he said between clenched

teeth. "I came to see your father because Randall needs your ad for this week's issue."

Georgina groaned. Her father was responsible for determining which items would go on sale, and then they would sit together to work out the design.

"I'm sorry, Langston, but my father is on vacation and he's not expected back until the end of the week. And that means I'm going to have to select the sale items and design the ad. How soon do you need it?"

"The final copy will have to be at the printer before nine Wednesday night."

She groaned again. "I'll stay after the store closes and work up one for you."

"Are you sure that's what you want to do?"

Georgina stared at Langston as if he'd suddenly taken leave of his senses. He'd come asking for the ad because he was on deadline, while in the same breath was questioning her. "Do you or don't you need the ad?"

"Yes, but not at the expense of you falling on your face. When was the last time you had a restful night's sleep?"

"I don't remember," she said truthfully. "I've been burning the candles at both ends running the store and packing up what I need to move into my new place."

Cupping her elbow, Langston steered her over to a rack with snacks, candy bars and mints. "Are you eating regularly?" he whispered.

"I do when I can."

"I'm coming over after you close to bring you something to eat and to help you with the ad."

"You don't have to do that, Langston. I can get something from Ruthie's."

"I'll get something from Ruthie's or the Den. The choice is yours," he said. There was a hint of finality in his voice.

Georgina glared up at him. "I don't need you taking care of me."

"Someone should, because if you continue burning the candles at both ends you're never going to survive long enough to enjoy your new home. You'll end up in the hospital from exhaustion."

"Why are you so concerned about my health?"

"I'm concerned, Georgi, because I like you. A lot," he added.

She didn't want to believe their spending a few hours together more than two weeks ago had elicited feelings in Langston that had him inviting her to his home and concerned for her well-being. A hint of a smile flitted over her expression of uncertainty. And despite her limited experience with the opposite sex, he was the first man, other than her father, who appeared genuinely interested in her welfare.

"Do you feed all the women you like?" she teased.

"Nah, because there aren't too many women that I like as much as you."

"Why me, Langston?"

He blinked. "Why not you? Do you believe you're unworthy for a man to care about you?"

"Of course not!" Her protest came out much too quickly for Georgina to even believe what she'd just confessed. She was aware she had a lot to offer a man but only if he would take the time to get to know and understand her and not relate to her as Powell's girl or daughter. She also wondered if they would get to see her differently once she left the department store to start up her own business.

"Good. Now, let me know what you'd like to eat, and I'll bring it by after seven."

Georgina knew it was futile to argue with Langston. Not when anyone within earshot could overhear them. "Surprise me. Send me a text and I'll come and open the back door."

He smiled, bringing her gaze to linger on his mouth. "Now, that wasn't so difficult, was it?"

She smiled when she didn't want to. "Now, go so I can finish some paperwork before I decide what to put on sale."

Langston sobered. "Do you feel safe staying here alone after the store closes?"

"Yes. I'll arm the alarm, which is wired directly to the sheriff's office."

"That's good to know."

Georgina stared at Langston's departing figure and when she looked at the two women at checkout she realized they also had been staring at him.

Girls in their neighborhood had always flirted with him, but to their disappointment he related to them like he had his sister. There was little or no interaction between her and Langston because he was older than she was. She and his sister Jacklyn shared a few classes but somehow, they never connected. Georgina had become fast friends with Sasha Manning, where they trusted each other with their heartfelt secrets.

She'd looked forward to leaving Wickham Falls to attend art school, while Sasha couldn't wait to graduate to escape her parents' dysfunctional relationship. Her friend left and returned as a successful pastry chef to open her own bakeshop, while Georgina had stayed and was now looking forward to opening her craft shop.

She walked up and down aisles searching for items to discount for sale. Easter was late this year and while they traditionally discounted Easter-themed candy after the holiday, Georgina decided to advertise them as pre-holiday items. She would further cut the price of chocolate bunnies, jellybeans and Peeps until they exhausted their inventory.

The success of the store came from the dedication of longtime employees. Many were hired within days of graduating high school, and elected to stay because of paid vacation and sick leave, and merit-based raises. Bruce had a policy that if you treated people well, then they would become loyal work-

ers. The store opened at nine and closed at seven
Monday through Saturday, and from noon to six on
Sundays. And in keeping with the town's tradition
that everyone should be given the opportunity to
participate in the three-day Fourth of July celebration, shopkeepers were given the option of closing
one day out of the three. Last year Bruce had closed
for all three because the Fourth fell on a Friday, and
reopened on Monday.

The Fourth of July and the Fall Frolic festivities
were her favorite holidays, and even if she'd moved
away, Georgina knew she would return to the Falls
year after year to celebrate with her townspeople.
She took out her phone from the pocket of her smock
and snapped photos of the sale items, and went back
to her office to finish what she'd been working on
before Langston arrived.

She consciously tried not to think about him, because when she did she'd found herself distracted as
she recalled what it felt like to be in his arms when
they'd danced together. Then there was the way that
he stared at her as if he could see beyond the fragile veneer of confidence she worked hard to project
whenever she found herself in the presence of a man
to whom she was attracted.

Georgina had convinced herself that becoming
involved with Langston would prove detrimental to
her emotional stability because she couldn't afford to
be distracted by romantic notions, and he was much

too attractive and virile to ignore for long periods of time. He was the total package: looks, intelligence and professionally successful.

She knew he was interested in her, but if she could keep him at bay until she felt confident that her business was viable, then she would be more than willing to become involved with him.

Georgina met the stockroom boy as he handed her a packing slip for a shipment of paper goods. "I checked off everything, Miss Powell."

"Thank you, Justin." Her father had hired the high school senior to work from three to closing. He proved to be a reliable employee, arriving on time to unpack boxes and stock shelves.

Every barcode was scanned into the computerized cash registers, and twice a week Georgina checked the inventory to determine which items needed to be reordered. Now that she looked back, she realized working full-time at the store for fourteen years had given her the experience and acumen needed to operate her own enterprise.

A ringtone on her cell phone indicated Georgina had a text message. Langston was at the back door. Everyone left minutes before seven and she'd locked the automatic front doors and activated the security gate that protected the interior of the property from intruders, and then set the alarm. There had been a time when the janitorial service arrived once the store closed, but Bruce had arranged for them to come between the hours of eight and nine to clean up because he hadn't wanted to stay behind to monitor them. They were bonded by their employer but that hadn't stopped the theft of housewares and small appliances. He canceled his contract with the company and hired a local man who'd retired as a custodian for the school system who now came in every morning to sweep the floors, clean the bathrooms and bag the trash and garbage.

Georgina punched in the code for the alarm and opened the door. Langston's slicker was drenched. It hadn't stopped raining. "Come in and dry off."

"I don't like getting wet."

She waited for him to walk in to close the door and rearm the system. "Why? Because you're so sweet you might melt like brown sugar?" she teased.

Langston set two shopping bags stamped with Ruthie's logo on the floor, then lowered his head and brushed his mouth over hers, deepening the kiss until she pushed against his chest. "Tell me, Sleepy Beauty. Am I sweet enough?"

Laughing, Georgina swatted at him as if he were an annoying insect. He reached for her again and she managed to sidestep him. "It's not Sleepy, but Sleeping Beauty. What happened to me being Cinderella?"

Winking at her, he picked up the bags. "You're that, too. You admit that you haven't had much sleep, so the prince thought he'd wake you up with a kiss."

He wanted to continue to kiss her, and she'd stopped him because she wasn't ready for whatever Langston would want from her. Would kisses be enough for him or would he want more? And if he did, then she wasn't ready for the more, which to her translated into them perhaps sleeping together.

She gave him a sidelong glance as she led the way to the break room. "But he only kisses her to wake her from the spell in which she would sleep for a hundred years."

"You really know your fairy tales, don't you?"

Georgina flashed a sexy smile. "You're not the only one whose mother read them fairy tales. But as I got older, I realized some of them were very scary with wolves attempting to eat little pigs, Red Riding Hood, and they are also filled with wicked witches and jealous stepmothers."

"I never thought of them like that." Langston paused. "Are you saying that if you have children you won't read fairy tales to them?"

Having children was something Georgina did not consciously think about. First, she had to get her life together before bringing another one into the world. "I probably will because kids nowadays aren't frightened of too many things. There are animated movies about friendly monsters, so I doubt if the characters from fairy tales will bother them. What I really like are nursery rhymes and stories from the Little Golden Books." Georgina smiled when she recalled happier days before she'd started school when her mother would allow her to crawl into bed with her, and she would beg Evelyn to read to her. "By the way, how much did you order?" she asked, deftly changing the topic from children.

Langston rested the bags on a folding chair and then removed his slicker and cap, hanging both on hooks attached to the wall. "Enough for tonight and leftovers for several days."

Georgina opened an overhead cabinet and took out plates, glasses and two bottles of water from the refrigerator. By the time she'd set the table, Langston had removed containers with roast chicken, steamed green beans, broccoli, carrots, rice, mashed potatoes, pickled beets, caprese and fried shrimp.

His head popped up. "There's chicken pot pie, beef stew, fried chicken and corn on the cob in the other bag."

"There's no way I'm going to be able to eat all this food even if I have it for breakfast, lunch and dinner. You're going to have to take some home with you."

"Are you going to come over and share it with me?" he asked.

Georgina bit her lip to smother a smile. "What's with you trying to get me to come to your house?"

Langston sobered. "I don't like eating alone."

"You need a girlfriend." The suggestion was out before Georgina could censor herself.

Langston lowered his eyes. Georgina had just verbalized what he'd been contemplating for several months now. He hadn't had a girlfriend since coming back to Wickham Falls, even though he'd dated a few women since his divorce yet hadn't felt at the time that he was ready for a relationship because his life wasn't exactly stable. He hadn't been certain whether he would continue to work for the television station but once he was subpoenaed to meet behind closed doors with a congressional committee about his book, Langston had had enough of reporting on wars, navigating DC rush-hour traffic and repeated requests to name his sources.

"You're probably right," he said after a pregnant pause. "Do you know any candidates?"

"Nope. But if I think of someone, I'll let you know. Should she have any particular qualities?"

Langston waited for Georgina to serve herself, then he served himself. "I prefer she be between the ages of thirty and forty. Her physical appearance isn't a deal breaker, but I would like her to be able to hold an intelligent conversation without her repeating the word *like* ten times in a sentence."

Georgina laughed. She knew exactly what he was talking about, because she'd noticed people peppering their speech with the word when making comparisons. "Anything else?"

"She should prefer men."

"What about dogs and kids?"

"I like dogs and kids, but not particularly in that

order," he said. "I'm less enthusiastic when it comes to cats. I have a friend who has the cat from hell. Every time I'd visit his house, that little furry sucker would come up behind me and rake a paw over the back of my head. I'm certain if I shave my head you'd see scars from her claws."

"What did you do to him?"

"It was a queen, and her name is Precious. But she was anything but precious, and I didn't do anything to her. She just didn't like me."

"That's where we differ, Langston. I happen to like cats because they are quiet and independent."

He speared a forkful of beets. "You like cats and I prefer dogs. Does this mean you are not in the running?"

"That's exactly what I'm saying, Mr. Cooper."

"What if I decide to take a liking to cats?"

Georgina shook her head. "Oh no, Langston. You're not going to pretend to like cats on my account. And besides, I don't have time for a boyfriend."

"Why not, Georgi?"

"Because right now I have much too much on my plate. I work seven days every other week, I'm moving and I'm working on samples to exhibit once I open my shop." Georgina closed her eyes, groaning. "Oops! I shouldn't have said that," she whispered.

Langston realized she'd made a faux pas, but it was too late for her to retract it. "You're going into business for yourself." The question was a statement. She opened her eyes, nodding. "Do you want to tell me about it?"

She exhaled a breath. "Only if it doesn't go beyond this room."

He gave her a long stare. "Any and everything you tell me is off the record."

Chapter Five

Georgina didn't want to believe a slip of the tongue would result in her revealing her plans to a man who made a living disseminating information. But she had to trust him, because he'd given his word. He would keep her secret.

"I decided to go into business for myself once my father downsized and then eliminated the store's arts and crafts section. I boxed up all of the merchandise and rented a storage unit."

"You're that proficient that you'll be able to give instructions?"

"Yes. My grandmother taught me to knit, crochet, quilt and the rudiments of embroidery and needle-point."

Langston's expression brightened. "I remember visiting my maternal grandmother in South Carolina during the summer recess and at the end of the day she'd sit on the porch and knit sweaters for me and my sister. Every Christmas she would send us knitted socks, gloves and scarfs."

"Handmade garments are a dying art, so that's why I want to open a shop catering to those who want to learn, and others that still knit, crochet and quilt."

"Will it be here in the Falls?" Langston asked, and she appeared startled by his query.

"Yes. I discovered there were a few vacant storefronts on Sheridan Street. I've already signed a lease with the landlord and submitted an application to the town's housing department for a permit for occupancy."

"How long do you project you'll have to wait for their approval?"

"I was told two months. What I don't understand, Langston, is why it takes so long for the town council to approve startups."

"There's a lot of bureaucratic red tape involved with a new company because of an intensive background investigation. I went through the same thing when I offered to buy the paper. What the council doesn't want is for someone to use a business as a front for illegal activity. Before I left for college I'd overheard my parents talking about the guy who'd opened the shoe store to launder money for a cousin who was trafficking in drugs and needed somewhere to hide his money. The IRS caught up with him when it was apparent he was depositing a lot more money than his reported income, and that alerted the mayor and the members of the town council so they decided not to fast-forward any future applications for new businesses."

Georgina angled her head. "I do remember the notice posted on his door because of a tax lien, but I can assure you I will not be laundering money for anyone."

"Do you feel confident running your own business?"

Georgina gave him a death stare. Did he believe because she was a woman she would fail? "What do you think I've been doing the past fourteen years? I can tell you off the top of my head every piece of merchandise we stock in this store. I'm also familiar with accounts payable and receivables, payroll and employee benefits. Every item has been scanned digitally with a barcode and I've developed a computerized inventory program with alerts when to reorder. So to answer your question, yes, Langston. I feel very confident running my own business."

He held up both hands in supplication. "I'm sorry it came out like that. What I meant to ask is do you think you'll get enough customers for it to remain viable?"

Her attitude changed, becoming more conciliatory. "Yes. When we had the arts and crafts section in the store they sold well, but then my dad decided to expand sporting goods with the increasing popularity of soccer. And there's talk the school's athletics department is forming a soccer team."

"How does he feel about you leaving Powell's?"

"He doesn't know yet."

"What!"

Georgina bit back a smile. Langston looked as if he'd been stabbed by a sharp object. "I'll let him know once my permit is approved."

"But doesn't he depend on you to help him manage the store?"

"Yes, but I'm not going to leave him without a backup, Langston. I've asked my cousin Sutton Reed to take over for me."

Langston leaned forward. "Has he agreed?"

This time she did laugh when she saw excitement light up his eyes. "Yes."

"Hot damn! Your father better get prepared for the groupies hanging around just to get a glimpse of Sutton."

Maybe because he was her cousin Georgina did not see Sutton like that. Yes, he was gorgeous, a baseball phenom who'd become rookie of the year, won several gold gloves and a batting crown title, World Series ring and two homerun derbies. His image had also appeared on several sports magazines during his celebrated career. He'd married his college sweetheart, but the union ended due to irreconcilable differences after eight years.

"I'm certain Dad won't mind more traffic if it translates into higher sales."

Langston smiled. "Whatever works. Maybe after he's settled in, can you ask him if he's amenable for me to interview him for the 'Who's Who' column?"

Georgina nodded, smiling. The media loved Sutton because not only did he make himself available to them, but he was also extremely photogenic and articulate. "Of course."

"When do you expect him to come back?"

"Not for another month. He's waiting to close on his Atlanta condo." Whenever Sutton returned to the Falls to visit with his aunt Evelyn, her mother came alive, lavishing him with attention.

Several minutes of silence passed before Langston said, "If you didn't work here, would you have left the Falls like so many other kids when they graduate high school?"

"Like yourself?"

He stared at his plate. "Yes, like myself." His head popped up. "Once I was hired as an intern at the news station, I couldn't come back because there was no way I could compare working for a local paper to an award-winning all-news cable network."

Georgina took a sip of water, meeting Langston's

eyes over the top of the bottle. "If I'd had a choice I would've left to go to art school."

His eyebrows lifted. "You wanted to be an artist?"

"An illustrator," she corrected. "I wanted to go into animation. The other alternative was to become a court artist."

"Why didn't you?"

"My brother died."

Langston sat straight. "How did that stop you from going to art school?"

She took another sip of water, and then told him about how Kevin's passing had impacted her family, watching intently as myriad expressions crossed his features. "My mother agreeing to go to Hawaii for a couple of weeks shocked me and Dad. I'm certain my decision to move out temporarily jolted her out of her malaise, but knowing Mom it may not last long. She has good and bad days."

"Do you believe she'll come back to work here?"

"I don't know," Georgina said. "I suppose we're going to take it one day at a time. I never had a child, so I don't know what it is to lose one, but I'd believed my mother would eventually accept the fact that Kevin was gone and never coming back."

"Grief affects everyone differently. Whether it's losing a loved one, or a divorce, those who are involved will never be the same."

"Please don't get me wrong, Langston. I miss my brother and there isn't a day when I don't think about

him, and while it took me a long time, I had to resign myself to the fact that he wasn't coming back."
Georgina didn't want to talk about her brother or
the impact of his death on her family, when it appeared as if a modicum of healing had begun with
her pronouncement that she was moving out. Now
Evelyn would be forced to lean on her husband for
companionship and emotional support rather than
her daughter.

"Do you still draw?"

She didn't know why, but Georgina felt as if
Langston was interviewing her for his "Who's Who"
column as he continued with his questioning. However, he'd promised everything she told him was off
the record—none of which would appear in the biweekly.

"No. It's been years since I've picked up a sketch
pad. I did a lot of sketching when I was on the high
school's newspaper committee. If you search the archives, you will see some of my caricatures."

"You must have joined the newspaper club after
I'd graduated."

"I did," she confirmed. "I waited until my junior
year to get involved. But I must admit as the former
editor of *The Mountaineer* you were a tough act to
follow. Mr. Murray reminded us constantly that you
had set a high bar when you were the editor, and that
some of our articles were so sophomoric that he was
ashamed to put out the issue."

"Murray fashioned himself a slave driver. He said the same thing to me and the others in the newspaper club, and it wasn't until I got into journalism school that I realized he was a pussycat compared to some of my professors."

Propping her elbow on the table, Georgina rested her chin on the heel of her hand. "Don't be so modest, Langston. I'd read some of your articles and they were exceptional. Just accept that you're a gifted writer. And when news of your first book was published, Dad ordered several cartons and convinced everyone who came into the store to buy a copy."

"I'd heard he was offering a fifteen percent discount on their total purchases if they bought the book."

Georgina made a sucking sound with her tongue and teeth. "Whatever works. I'm certain we sold enough copies to boost your sales, so you were able to make a bestseller list. You can't say the Falls' folks don't stick together."

"That was one of the several reasons why I'd decided to come back here to live."

"Why did you come back?" Georgina asked him.

Langston chose his words carefully when he said, "I wanted to go to bed and not wake up to the sounds of honking horns, the wailing sirens from emergency vehicles, explosions or the exchange of gunfire. I believed I'd gotten used to the noise and hustle of New

York City when I went to college, but it was nothing compared to covering a war as a correspondent."

Georgina lowered her arm. "How long were your assignments?"

"Too long, Georgi. Now I know how soldiers feel when they're deployed. The only thing you look forward to is the next sunrise."

She blinked slowly. "Do you have PTSD?"

Langston stared over her shoulder at the counter-top with a microwave, single-serve coffeemaker and toaster oven. "Yes."

"Have you seen a therapist?"

"Yes," he repeated. "The flashbacks don't occur as often as they had in the past. I've had only two since I've been back."

"Hopefully, one day they'll disappear completely." There was a hint of wistfulness in her voice.

"That's what I'm hoping," he said, although he doubted whether certain atrocities he'd witnessed he would ever forget.

"You stay and finish your dinner while I pull up an ad for you."

"Do you need my assistance?"

She stood. "I don't think so. I save all of our ads on the computer so I just have to find a file with Easter items and revise or update it."

Langston rose with her. "If you don't mind, I'll clean up here."

"I don't mind. Just scrape and rinse the dishes before you put them in the dishwasher."

"Yes, ma'am."

He waited for Georgina to leave to clear the table. It was the second time they'd spent time together and just her presence reminded him how long it had been since he was able to have an intelligent conversation with a woman with whom he'd found himself interested.

When she'd suggested he get a girlfriend his intent was to tell her she would be his first choice. Langston told her a woman's looks did not matter because he didn't want her to think of him as shallow.

He was transfixed by Georgina's bare face with a sprinkling of freckles across her nose and her hair fashioned in a single braid, and equally enthralled with the transformation with a subtle cover of makeup and the absence of curls in a sophisticated twist.

She'd shocked him when she'd revealed she was opening a business in the Falls. Georgina would become the second woman in less than six months who would become a business owner, of which there were too few in a town of more than four thousand residents.

Dr. Henry Franklin retired from his family practice and it was now run by Philadelphia transplant Dr. Natalia Hawkins-Collier. Pastry chef Sasha Manning had returned home to open Sasha's Sweet

Shoppe to much success. Bessie Daniels owned Perfect Tresses, and now Georgina would be added to the list of women business owners when she opened her craft shop.

He'd left Wickham Falls at eighteen to attend college and had returned at thirty-six and only a few things had changed during his absence. His parents retired, sold the pharmacy and moved permanently to their Key West vacation home.

His parents said repeatedly that they had the best boss in the world—themselves. After graduating with degrees in pharmacology, his father went to work in a hospital pharmacy, while his mother got a position with a chain store pharmacy. After several years they'd decided to go into business for themselves, which allowed them to make their own hours and control their future. It had taken Langston many more years than his parents had, but he was now his own boss. Jacklyn had also followed in their parents' footsteps when she left teaching to become a writer. He had finished cleaning up the break room at the same time Georgina returned.

She handed him a printout of the ad. "I just downloaded a copy to the paper."

A chuckle rumbled in his chest before it exploded in an unrestrained laugh. "This is incredibly cute." The ad had tiny bunnies, and baby chicks spelling out the department store's logo and bold lettering advertising pre-Easter discounts on candy and decorations.

Georgina flashed a smug grin. "I'm glad you like it."

"Did you design this?"

"Yes."

He gave her a sidelong glance. "I thought you said you didn't sketch anymore."

"I don't. I'm sorry to disappoint you, but I have templates of all kinds of images and I highlight what I want and then transfer them to an ad or flier."

Langston wanted to ask Georgina who was being modest now. Not only did she have an exceptionally creative mind, but she also had an incredible eye for detail. "This is the most eye-catching ad you've sent us."

"Thank you."

"No, Georgi, thank you. You're very talented."

She exhibited what passed for a smile. "Well, this very talented tired shopkeeper is about to head home so she can get some sleep before getting up to come back to this rodeo." Georgina pointed to the containers on the table. "Please take those with you."

"What if I leave them for your employees?"

"What if you don't?" she countered. "The ladies are on restricted diets and I don't want them to accuse me of trying to sabotage them."

"I can't eat all of this food."

"Now you sound like me. What if I come to your

house tomorrow after I close, and I'll help you put a dent in this mini banquet?"

Langston felt as if he'd won a small victory. He hadn't invited Georgina to his house to come on to her but to prove to himself that he could regain a sense of normalcy that had evaded him far too long. Before moving back to the Falls he'd closed himself off from friends and former colleagues who he'd meet after work for happy hour or invite to his condo during football season.

His therapist had recommended he get out of his apartment or invite some of the guys who worked for the station over to watch a game, but he had resisted because he feared having them witness a flashback. None of them were aware he was afflicted with PTSD. Inviting employees to his home was not an option, but Georgina wasn't his employee but someone with whom he felt comfortable enough to be forthcoming.

"Text me and let me know when I should expect you. Now, I'll wait for you to lock up and then we'll leave together."

Georgina did not want to think of going to Langston's house to eat as a date, but based on her experience with men it was to her. She couldn't keep a steady boyfriend once they discovered she still lived with her parents. Her relationship with Sean was the exception because she always drove to Beckley to see him. Perhaps she'd been naive when she had overlooked the signs that told her Sean wasn't what he presented. Most times he paid for their dates, but occasionally, he'd claim he'd overspent and asked her to cover the check. However annoying, it hadn't happened so often that alarm bells went off in her head that her boyfriend had a problem managing his finances. She'd continued to see him because he'd charmed her parents, and her father liked the fact that she was dating a man whose family was also successful business owners.

They'd even talked about marriage and debating where they would live while both continued to oversee their respective family enterprises; her so-called fairy-tale romance ended abruptly when Sean called her in a panic, begging her to meet him at his house later that night.

She'd driven to Beckley, her pulse pounding an accelerated rhythm as she tried imagining what had upset him. Once he revealed his dilemma Georgina felt as if she'd been stabbed through her heart. The man with whom she'd fallen in love and contemplated marriage was addicted to gambling. He'd pleaded with her to lend him the money because not only did he need to cover the fifteen thousand he'd embezzled from the dealership, but he also owed his bookie more than five thousand dollars. She'd experienced twin emotions of shock and disappointment. Shocked that she'd fallen in love with a gambler, and disappointed that yet again a man was only interested in her bank balance.

Although she did not regard herself as wealthy, she was far from being labeled a pauper. She lived at home, and therefore she did not have to pay for housing; her closet wasn't filled with designer labels because her social life was nonexistent. And her only big-ticket item was an automobile, which she never financed. Georgina knew it was the future possibility of her assuming complete control of Powell's that had folks viewing her as the golden goose.

She'd shown no emotion when she wished Sean luck and if his bookie followed through with his threat then she was certain his mother would let her know where to send flowers: to the hospital or funeral home. However, she did promise him that she wouldn't tell anyone about his addiction. Georgina returned to Wickham Falls devastated and told her mother why she'd decided to break up with Sean. Evelyn claimed it was all for the best, and that she would get over his duplicity faster by throwing all her energies into Powell's.

Georgina removed her smock, leaving it on a coatrack, and left her office. She approached longtime employee Diana Kelly. "Mrs. Kelly, I have to leave for a while, so I'd like you to cover the front for me."

The middle-aged grandmother's quick smile and friendly greeting to everyone who came into Powell's had made her a favorite go-to clerk and an invaluable employee. "Of course, sweetie." Everyone was *sweetie* to the petite, dark-skinned woman with short, natural hair.

Georgina chided herself for not putting on a jacket over her long-sleeve tee when she left the store and walked along Main Street to Sasha's Sweet Shoppe. The rain had finally stopped but not even the bright spring sunlight could dispel the unseasonal chill in the air. She quickened her pace and opened the door to the bakeshop, the bell chiming and announcing someone had come in. Within seconds Charlotte Manning came from the rear of the store. Charlotte had stepped in to help her daughter when she volunteered to manage the bakeshop for the morning shift, while Kiera Adams, the dentist's teenage daughter, worked the afternoons.

"What brings you in so early?" Charlotte Manning asked, smiling. The widowed, fifty-something woman with silvered blond hair and brilliant blue eyes hadn't lost any of her youthful beauty.

"I came to ask Sasha for advice about what type of dessert I could bring to someone's home for dinner."

"Go on back. Right now Sasha is decorating cupcakes."

Although she and Sasha shared many classes in high school, their friendship did not extend to sleepovers. Sasha had confided to her that her parents argued constantly, and she wanted what went on in the Manning household to remain behind closed doors; all three Manning kids left home within weeks of graduating.

"Hey, friend," Georgina crooned when Sasha's net-covered head popped up. "Oh, my word! Those decorations are awesome!"

Sasha set down the piping bag and removed a pair of disposable gloves. "I use Russian piping tips to create leaves and colorful flowers. I'm able to decorate dozens in less than a half hour."

"They look too pretty to eat." Delicate green leaves surrounded circles of vibrant pink and red roses.

"I try to take them to the next level."

"You more than try, Sasha. Everyone's talking about the deliciousness coming out of this shop and I can see why. It's like Willie Wonka's. Instead of chocolate it's cupcakes and cookies."

Sasha sat on a stool and patted the one next to her. "Sit down, Georgi, and tell me what you want."

She stared at the naturally curly strawberry-blond woman with emerald-green eyes, silently admiring her friend who'd turned heads at the Chamber fund-raiser. Georgina knew it wasn't only from what she'd been wearing but also because she'd attended as Dwight Adams's date.

"I know this is short notice, but I'm going to someone's home for dinner tonight, and I'd like a suggestion what I can bring as dessert."

Sasha pushed her hands into the pockets of the pink smock. "How many people will be at the dinner?"

"Just two."

A smile played at the corners of the chef's mouth. "Should I assume the other person is a man?"

Georgina smiled. "Yes. It's Langston Cooper."

Throwing back her head, Sasha laughed loudly. "When I saw you two together at the fund-raiser, I told Dwight that Langston was—what's the word they use in romance novels when the hero falls hard for the heroine?"

"Besotted."

Sasha snapped her fingers. "Yes, that's it. He was totally besotted with you."

Georgina wanted to tell her friend she was wrong. Although he'd given her a chaste kiss and alluded to her becoming his possible girlfriend, she didn't get the vibe that he was serious. "And Dr. Adams isn't besotted with you?" she countered.

"No. Our only connection is that his daughter works for me."

"If you say so, Sasha."

"You don't believe me?"

"No, I don't. You haven't been back long enough to know that a lot of women are willing to give up their eyeteeth to get Dwight Adams to notice them."

Sasha laughed again. "I can't believe you have dentist jokes." She sobered. "Now, back to you and Langston. What are you looking for?"

"Something that is not too sweet."

"I can put together a box of miniature red velvet brownies and petit fours."

Georgina passed her palms together. "That sounds perfect. How much do I owe you?"

"Nothing," Sasha said as she slipped off the stool. "I don't charge my friends for their first order. The exception is a wedding cake."

"Bite your tongue, my friend. You know I'm nowhere ready to become someone's wife. Thanks to you, I'm planning to move into my own place, and it will be the first time in my life that I'll be totally on my own." Smiling, she stood. "And right now I'm a little too selfish to share me with anyone on a permanent basis."

"You don't have to thank me, Georgi. Don't forget I cried on your shoulder every week about what was going on in my home when we were in school together. You were the one who told me that I had options. That I could enlist in the military or find a position in another city or state."

Sasha had taken her advice and left Wickham Falls; she'd enrolled in culinary school, becoming a pastry chef, then a contestant in a televised baking competition, which set the stage for her baking for celebrities, and she'd also married A-list country superstar Grant Richards. Now Sasha had come full circle. She'd relocated from Nashville after divorcing her husband to start over in Wickham Falls.

"I'll come over later to pick it up."

"Don't bother, Georgi. I'll have my mother drop it off at the end of her shift."

Georgina hugged Sasha. "We have to get together whenever I'm settled in my new digs."

Sasha pressed her cheek to Georgina's. "That's a bet."

She returned to Powell's, thanked Mrs. Kelly for filling in for her and answered a customer's question about which mandolin was best for zesting. Aside from the arts and crafts section, she liked housewares best, and Georgina was looking forward to the time when she would be able to prepare her own meals in the guesthouse kitchen.

The morning and afternoon passed quickly and when the programmed recorded announcement echoed through the store it would be closing in ten minutes, Georgina knew she had to get home, shower and dress for her dinner date with Langston.

Chapter Six

Langston stood on the porch, waiting for Georgina's arrival. She'd sent him a text indicating she was on her way. Although they lived within walking distance, he rarely got to see Georgina when they were growing up, and he attributed that to the four-year difference in their ages. She and his sister shared several classes, however they never connected to become more than classmates.

Headlights swept over other cars parked in the cul-de-sac and he smiled when her off-white SUV came closer. Coming down off the porch, Langston motioned for Georgina to park behind the classic Mustang that had once belonged to his father. Over the years, Annette Cooper had accused her husband of loving the muscle car more than her and any of their children and had convinced him to gift it to Langston rather than transport the vehicle to Florida. Langston had contacted Jesse Austen, who owned and operated the only auto repair shop in Wickham Falls for decades, to tow the car to his garage for a complete overhaul. And the result was the forty-year-old vehicle ran like new.

He opened the driver's-side door after Georgina came to a complete stop and cut off the engine. A smile softened his features when she placed her palm on his as he assisted her down. A ponytail had replaced the ubiquitous braid, a cascade of curls floating halfway down her back over a ruffled white silk blouse. He thought she looked incredibly feminine in the blouse she'd paired with stretchy black slacks and matching ballet flats. Langston inhaled her perfume, a scent that had lingered with him hours after the fund-raiser ended, and he'd found the fragrance as unique as its wearer. It wasn't flowery, but slightly woodsy with notes of patchouli and vanilla.

He dipped his head and pressed a kiss to her cheek. "Thank you for coming."

"Thank you for the invite."

Georgina's smoky voice caressed his ear, reminding him why he liked talking with her. The timbre was low, hypnotic and controlled. Even when annoyed, her tone did not change.

"I decided to change the menu."

"To what?" she asked.

"Come inside and you'll see."

"I brought dessert. It's on the passenger seat."

Langston rested a hand at the small of her back. "I'll get it. Please go inside, Georgi. I've got this."

Georgina walked up the porch steps and into the house where Langston and his sister Jacklyn had grown up. The farmhouse style was like hers and others in the upscale neighborhood designed by the same architect/builder nearly fifty years ago. All two-story structures were advertised with four bedrooms, three baths, formal living and dining rooms, full basement, two-car garages and wraparound porches. Unlike her house, the Cooper property was in a cul-de-sac with no access for through traffic.

Growing up she'd found it odd that the residents in the enclave usually kept to themselves. The exception was when someone passed away, then they all came together to support the survivors. They preferred joining local civic organizations when it came to socializing with one another. Georgina's mother had participated in the church's semiannual food drive, Toys for Tots and had been an active member in the Chamber of Commerce. After burying Kevin, she rarely left the house, and when she did it was to sporadically attend church services or drop by the store. Georgina wished her father had told her sooner, rather than later, about her mother's inability to have more children, which would've made Evelyn's behavior much more tolerable.

The entryway appeared to be a desert oasis with tables of varying heights cradling decorative pots filled with a variety of succulents. Bright red flowers sprouted from the saguaro in a large copper planter. She felt the heat from Langston's body as he came up behind her.

"How often do you water these beauties?"

"Once a month. These were my mother's pride and joy and she wanted to take them with her to Florida, but Dad talked her out of it because the bungalow is very small. It's no bigger than a studio apartment I'd once rented in New York City. By the way, you didn't need to bring dessert, but I'm not going to refuse anything that comes from Sasha's patisserie."

Georgina smiled at Langston over her shoulder. "Did you know she wanted to call the bakeshop Sasha's Patisserie, but decided against it because she thought most folks wouldn't understand what the word meant?"

"We mountaineers aren't that uninformed," Langston said defensively.

"Please, don't get me wrong, Langston, because as a fellow mountaineer we definitely aren't ignorant. You know what patisserie means because you've spent at least half your life traveling to different countries, while many from the Falls have barely left the state."

Langston reached for her hand. "One of these days I'll tell you about some of the countries I've visited."

"Was it for work?"

"Not all of them. There were some countries I always wanted to see, and being stationed abroad made it easier to take side trips."

Georgina entered the living room and saw firsthand why the Coopers had decided to retire to Key West, Florida. As a student of art, she recognized Caribbean island influences with rich mahogany carved pieces, a mixing of rattan and woven furniture, with an emphasis on plants. The influence stemming from France, Spain, Holland and Demark, all vying for control of the many islands, was apparent in the furnishings in the formal dining room with a Regency-style table with Jamaican rope-style legs. The table was set for two with plates, silver and crystal.

"Your home is beautiful." She couldn't hide the awe in her voice.

"I'll let Mom know you admire her decorating skill."

Georgina wanted to tell Langston that his mother's decorating skill went beyond someone who knew what she liked. The items she'd chosen to decorate her home were comparable to those selected by professional interior decorators. "Did it bother her that she had to leave all this when she relocated?"

Langston nodded. "Yes. Dad used to call me several times a week complaining that Mom wanted to sell the Key West bungalow and buy a larger house so she could transport the furniture in this place to their new residence. There was no way Dad was going to trade one four-bedroom house for another at his age. The impasse ended when I told him once I sold my DC condo I'd buy this house and with the furnishings, which pacified Mom. Decorating the rooms in this house had become her passion, and whenever she had time off she would call antiques shops to ask if they had a particular lamp, table or bed."

"With her eye for detail, she definitely could have a second career as a decorator."

Langston laughed softly. "After forty years as a pharmacist, all my mother wants to do is kick back and relax. She and Dad are so laidback that they don't have any clocks in the house. They even turned off the one on the microwave."

"Do you intend to follow in their footsteps once you retire, Langston?"

"I don't know. I'm thirty-six, so I have at least another thirty years before I can plan for my retirement. What about you, Georgi? Have you thought about what you'd like to do once you retire?"

Turning, Georgina looked up at Langston staring down at her. Wearing flats made her aware of the differences in their heights. She stood five six in bare feet, and he towered over her by at least another six inches. "After coming back from vacationing in some exotic locale where the only strenuous thing I'd have to do is raise my hand for a waiter to bring me more food and drink, I'd sit on the porch knitting sweaters and hats for my grandchildren."

Throwing back his head, Langston laughed with abandon. "Now that sounds as if you're not going to exert much energy whether on vacation or sitting on the porch," he teased.

"That's because I'm going to put all of my energy into running my business, where I will be entitled to take it easy once I decide to retire."

"Should I assume marriage and children will figure into your equation?"

Georgina shrugged her shoulders under the frilly blouse. "If it happens, Langston. And if it doesn't, then it's not going to be the end of the world for me. A lot of women go through life unmarried and childless and live wonderful, fulfilled lives."

"You're right about that," he said in agreement. "I've worked with a lot of women who prefer career to marriage and motherhood."

"Do you admire them for that?" Georgina questioned.

"Whether I do or don't is irrelevant. I believe because we all have an expiration date, folks should do whatever they want, because life can be totally unpredictable and to wait may not be best for them."

"Do you want to get married again, and maybe this time have children?"

His mother had asked him the same question and he'd told her no, because at the time his head was so mixed up, he hadn't known what he wanted to do at that moment or even the next day. But Georgina wasn't his mother and he was now in a better place mentally and emotionally.

"I've been thinking about it."

"How long do you plan to think about, Langston? Either you do or you don't."

Suddenly, he felt as if he was being cross-examined about something of which he had no knowledge. "I do." The two words came out unbidden.

Georgina patted his shoulder. "There you go. That wasn't so difficult to admit."

His eyebrows lifted slightly. "Are you in the running to become Mrs. Langston Wayne Cooper?"

"Surely you jest, Langston. I told you before I don't have time for a boyfriend and even less for a husband."

"But you're not opposed to marriage?"

She frowned. "I never said I didn't want to get married. Just not now."

Langston realized now that she was taking control of her life she would be more amenable to the things women her age wanted and looked forward to experiencing. He put his arm around her waist. "Come with me to the kitchen and I'll show you what I've prepared for dinner."

"What about the food from Ruthie's?" she asked.

"It will keep. I put them in vacuum-sealed bags that will go from the freezer to boiling water."

"You're really domesticated, aren't you?"

He winked at her. "You don't know the half."

Georgina let out an audible gasp when she saw the tray of ravioli on a parchment-covered cookie sheet. "You made ravioli."

Langston set the small white box stamped with tiny cupcakes on the countertop. "You said you like them, so I decided they would be better than eating leftovers."

Going on tiptoe, Georgina brushed a kiss over his mouth. "Thank you."

"You're most welcome."

"Where did you learn to make them?"

"That's a long story, Georgi."

"Well, we have until midnight before I have to leave, so I'm all ears."

Langston dropped a kiss on her curly hair when he wanted to kiss her mouth, if only to let her know of his deepening feelings for her. He'd told himself that he liked Georgina Powell, when in truth what he was beginning to experience went beyond a liking to wanting to spend uninterrupted hours with her, telling her things he had never told any other woman, including his ex-wife, because she'd proven not to be judgmental. When he'd admitted to experiencing PTSD, she hadn't asked him about his flashbacks but whether he had sought a therapist. He'd encountered worldly women, from every walk of life, some who interested him and others he couldn't wait to get away from. What he'd found ironic was he had to come back to his hometown to find himself attracted to one who appealed to something deep inside him. Under the veneer of being a world traveler and bestselling author, he was still a small-town dude who needed a woman similar to him in which to live his best life.

"I'll tell you everything over dinner."

Georgina sat across the table from Langston as she ate melt-in-the mouth little pockets of homemade pasta filled with butternut squash, Asian-infused shrimp, pork and spinach with feta in a delicious vodka sauce. He'd grilled marinated rib lamb chops and the seasonings of finely minced garlic and mint tantalized her palate. A mixed green salad with a ginger balsamic vinaigrette complemented the meat and pasta dishes. She'd drunk sparkling water in lieu of wine because she feared sleeping past the time when she had to get up in time to open the store.

"You missed your calling, Langston. You should've become a chef rather than a journalist."

Light from an overhead chandelier reflected off the sprinkling of gray in his cropped hair. "It was because I wanted to become a journalist that I learned to cook, not the other way around."

"I noticed a lot of Asian spices in the ravioli."

"That's because one of my college roommates came from China."

"How many roommates did you have?" she asked.

"Two. We'd rented a three-bedroom apartment in a walkway about five blocks from Columbia University. Joe Chen and Nicolas Rossi were exchange students from China and Italy who were also majoring in journalism. We didn't have a lot of money, so we'd pool our money and cook for ourselves. What was ironic was that Joe's and Nicolas's grandmothers had given them recipes of dishes they could make themselves, while my mother gifted me with a cookbook of recipes written by Southern church ladies.

"Nicolas had an aversion to store-bought pasta, so he made his own. And when Joe couldn't find the ingredients he needed for his dishes, we'd all hop on the subway and go downtown to Chinatown. Once I introduced them to Southern cuisine it was all she wrote. The apartment would smell like fried chicken and collard greens, or fried fish and grits for days until we were forced to open the windows when cooking even in the dead of winter."

Georgina smiled at him over the rim of her water glass. "It sounds as if you had a lot of fun."

"At the time I didn't know it would be one of the best times in my life. We were serious students, which meant there wasn't a steady stream of women coming and going at odd hours. Dad would deposit money in my checking account at the end of each month and if I didn't stick to my budget and ran out of money before the next deposit, then I was what you would call assed-out. I did get a part-time job at a Harlem restaurant waiting tables on the weekends and when I affected my best Southern accent the ladies suddenly would become very generous tippers. After a while I had regulars who'd ask for Country's table."

Georgina gave him an incredulous stare. "They called you *Country*?"

"Yes, ma'am."

"Were you flirting with them?"

"I plead the Fifth."

"Langston!"

He laughed. "Don't look so put out."

"Please don't tell me you were a naughty boy."

"The only thing I'm going to admit is that I was just naughty enough to make enough spare change to buy a ticket to a Broadway play or pay the cover charge at a jazz club."

Langston had no idea he'd gone up several points on Georgina's approval scale, because he was willing to work for what he wanted. Although his parents paid his college tuition, his portion of the rent on his Manhattan apartment and extra money for living expenses, he'd wanted more and worked as a waiter to subsidize the more.

"Did you enjoy living in New York?" Georgina asked as she cut into a piece of tender lamb, and then popped it into her mouth. Langston wasn't just good; he was an exceptional cook. It was apparent he and his college roommates ate very well.

"It took some getting used to. Even though we lived on the fourth floor I could still hear traffic and the wail of sirens from emergency vehicles. I was rest broken for the first few weeks before the noise lulled me to sleep. What I really enjoyed was spending the Christmas holiday in the city with all the lights and decorations."

"Do you think you could live there again?"

"No," Langston said without hesitating.

"What about DC?"

His expression changed, becoming a mask of stone. "I don't think I'll ever be able to live in a cosmopolitan city again."

Georgina knew it was time for her to stop probing into Langston's life when she saw hardness settle into his handsome features. It was obvious she'd asked him about something he'd rather not talk about or even forget. "It is apparent you haven't lost any of your cooking skills because dinner is delicious."

Langston inclined his head. "I'm glad you enjoyed it."

"I doubt whatever I'll make can come close to this."

"Why don't you let me be the judge of that?" he countered.

"I hope whenever I invite you over that you won't judge me too harshly."

He stared at her across the space under lowered lids. "If you hung out with your grandmother who taught you to knit and crochet, I'm certain she also taught you to cook."

Georgina touched the napkin to the corners of her mouth. "You're right about that. I loved going to Grandma Dot's house because she always had something simmering on the stove. She believed in making one-pot meals and whenever she made beef stew, pot roast, oxtails with ham hocks, fresh or smoked neck bones, she could count on me staying for dinner. My personal favorite of hers was smothered pork chops."

Langston groaned as if in pain. "Oh no, you didn't say smothered pork chops."

She smiled as he licked his lips. "Yes, I did."

Placing a hand over his heart, Langston shook his head. "I haven't had them in *years-s-s*." The last word came out in several syllables. "I've tried to eat healthy, but diet be damned for pork chops with gravy."

"When was the last time you had them?" Georgina asked.

Langston appeared deep in thought. "I can't remember."

"Are you ready to indulge for old times' sake?"

He narrowed one eye. "What are you hatching in that beautiful head of yours?"

Georgina did not visibly react to his calling her beautiful, because she didn't want to read more into the adjective than necessary. He hadn't only admitted it, but she was able to read between the lines when he'd revealed his intent to turn on the charm with women to earn tips.

"One of these days when I make smothered pork chops, you're welcome to come over and eat to your fill."

Langston pressed his palms together in a prayerful gesture. "Thank you."

Georgina had just made it easy for him to see her again. He did not want to come on too strong, turn her off, or pressure her to feel obligated to date him. He still wasn't certain what it was about Georgina, other than her overall physicality, that had drawn him to her, and he could not believe he'd traveled the world, encountered countless beautiful women from all races and ethnic backgrounds, yet he had come home to discover one who'd grown up and still lived literally in his backyard. Langston was aware that he did not have a type when it came to women. The only requisite was the ability to talk to each other.

He and his ex-wife had connected immediately because of her outspokenness. She'd let him know what she thought and felt and that if she hadn't been involved with another man she would've slept with him. Langston was shocked and flattered by her aggressiveness when she asked for his number with a promise that she would contact him once she broke up with her current boyfriend.

He'd forgotten about the aspiring off-Broadway actress until she called him a year later to let him know she was no longer in a relationship. He and Ayanna had been dating for three months when he received an assignment to travel to an African country to cover an upcoming election between a longtime president and a London-educated lawyer who'd returned after being exiled for six years. Langston had proposed marriage, Ayanna accepted and a week later they exchanged vows at a Bronx courthouse with one of her cast mates and his colleague as witnesses.

Covering the election was the first of many overseas assignments once the chief of the cable station's foreign news bureau recalled Langston's facility with languages. He had minored in Middle Eastern languages and had become fluent in Arabic, Farsi, Persian, Urdu, Hebrew and Dari—the most spoken language in Afghanistan. He'd also picked up Mandarin and Italian from his college roommates. When people asked him how he'd become a polyglot, Langston explained that something in his brain switched on when hearing another language other than English and after a while he had the ability to recall enough words and phrases to communicate with the locals. The gift had become a blessing and a curse after he'd published his second novel.

Divorcing Ayanna, resigning his position at the news station, selling his condo and severing ties with his literary agent were now a part of his past. He'd returned to Wickham Falls after a sixteen-year absence, purchased his parents' home, bought the failing biweekly, all with the intent of starting over. And Langston hadn't thought when he was assigned to a table at the Chamber's fund-raiser he would encounter someone with whom he'd rarely exchanged a word and that she would enthrall him as no other woman had, including his ex.

When he'd asked Georgina where she planned to open her shop she seemed almost shocked that he believed she would consider anyplace else. In that instant Langston knew they were kindred spirits. She'd spent her entire life in the Falls, and she did not plan to abandon it when starting up a new business.

He'd come back not to work for a local daily or television station but to attempt to resurrect a biweekly that had been the voice for Wickham Falls for generations. Editors had come and gone; some willing to challenge local government to do their elected duty to right the wrongs, while others pocketed money to circumvent the truth. As the current editor for *The Sentinel*, he owed it to his hometown to only print the truth.

"How much would you charge me if I commissioned you to knit a pullover sweater for my five-year-old nephew?" Langston asked after a comfortable silence.

"It would depend on the type of yarn and how long it would take me to knit it."

"Give me an example."

"If the instructions call for three skeins of bulky yarn at eight dollars per skein, and would take ten hours to knit and complete the garment, then I would charge you two hundred forty dollars."

Langston quickly did the math. "You're saying you'd multiply the cost of the materials by the number of hours to finish the sweater to arrive at the final figure?"

"Yes. The number of hours could vary appreciably if the instructions have a particular pattern with different colors, then of course this would increase the time spent and affect the total fee."

"How much time in advance do you need to knit a garment?"

Georgina's eyes studied him with curious intensity. "Do you want me to knit something for your nephew?"

"I'm thinking about it."

"Don't think too long, Country, because once I

have my grand opening I'm not going to have much free time for private customers."

Biting his lip, Langston slowly shook his head. "Something told me not to tell you about that."

"But you are country, Langston."

"And you're not?" he countered, grinning.

"Heck, yeah," Georgina admitted. "I'm a country girl down to the marrow in my bones, and I'm not ashamed to admit it."

"Well, Miss Country, my nephew will turn six on Halloween and I think he'd love to wear a holiday-themed sweater to school on his birthday."

"You're in luck because I have a book of children's holiday sweaters and I may be able to find one with Halloween. If not, then I'll make up a pattern."

"How would you do that?"

"I use graph paper and color in the boxes to correspond with the different color yarns. I prefer knitting the designs in the garment than appliquéing it. I could also crochet the sweater, which takes less time than knitting, but the flipside is that in crocheting I'll use much more yarn."

Suddenly, Langston saw Georgina's needlework skills in a whole new light. It was a lot more complicated than he thought. "I'll ask my sister what he likes about Halloween and then I'll let you know what she says."

Georgina looked back at him for a long moment and then said, "You're very special, because you'll become my first customer even before I open the front door."

Langston wanted to be special to her for a reason other than he'd asked her to make a handmade sweater. "Do you have a name for your shop?"

Her smile was dazzling. "Yes. It's A Stitch at a Time."

Reaching across the table he extended his fist, and he wasn't disappointed when Georgina gave him a fist bump. "Girl, you're on fire!" Leaning back in her chair, Georgina flashed a smile he interpreted as supreme confidence. She may have been denied going to art school, but with her patience and determination Langston knew instinctually that she was going to become a successful businesswoman.

It was close to ten when Langston walked Georgina to her car and waited for her to drive away. He'd spent more than two delightful hours with her, and again it wasn't enough. He had waited a year before welcoming a woman into what had become his sanctuary and the wait was worth it, because Wickham Falls was too small, and he too recognizable for him to have women coming and going like Union Station.

And once this week's paper was delivered to subscribers the photographs from the fund-raiser would take up the entire centerfold, and he knew tongues would start wagging with the candid photos of his interaction with Georgina. And judging from their smiles and body language they were into each other.

Although he'd told Jonas he did not care if folks talked about him, he did wonder how Georgina would react to the images of them together as what could be interpreted as a romantic couple. Langston couldn't stop people from drawing their own conclusions, yet he didn't want to place Georgina in a position where she would be forced to explain or defend her actions.

He decided to wait until the paper was out and then wait for her to contact him. If she didn't, then neither would he broach the subject.

Chapter Seven

Georgina walked into the kitchen Sunday morning to find her parents sitting in the breakfast nook flipping through back issues of *The Sentinel*. Their flight had landed Friday evening; they complained about experiencing jet lag and went directly to bed and slept through the night and into the following afternoon. It was apparent her father had gotten too much sun as evidenced by the peeling skin on his face and head, while her mother looked rested and content.

"I thought you guys would still be napping," she said, cheerfully.

Bruce smiled at her. "I decided to get up and go into the store today."

"Are you sure that's what you want to do, Dad?" Georgina asked him. Although it was his Sunday to work, she'd decided to step in and give him time to recover from his vacation.

"Yes. It's only six hours and if I hang around the house, I'll go stir-crazy."

Evelyn glanced up over her reading glasses. "Bruce, the store is not going to fall down if you don't go in."

"You tell him, Mom. It didn't fall apart when you guys were gone."

"I'm still going in," Bruce said under his breath as he walked out of the kitchen.

Georgina threw up a hand. "Mom, please talk to your husband."

Evelyn took off her glasses. "I'm going to do better than that. I'm going in with him and when he falls and hits his hard head, I'm going to call the EMTs and tell them to take him to the county hospital for observation. Your daddy doesn't know how to slow down and relax."

She had to agree with Evelyn. Her father ate, slept and breathed Powell's, and he did believe it would fall apart if he wasn't there to oversee it. And Georgina did not want to believe her mother had planned to go into the store. Perhaps going away had given Evelyn time to reflect on how she'd been living her life, cut off from the outside world, while she'd continued to dwell on the past.

"Do you want me to cook something that will last you for a few days?"

Evelyn shook her head. "No. It's been a while since your father and I have gone out for dinner. You've done enough while we were gone, and now it's time for you to relax."

Georgina smiled. "Thanks, Mom."

Now that she didn't have to go to work, she planned to go to the supermarket and shop for groceries to take to the guesthouse. She'd also bought a set of cookware and kitchen utensils she wanted to use when preparing her meals.

Evelyn returned her smile. "I see from the photographs in *The Sentinel* that you and Langston look like a real couple. I'm sorry I didn't get to see you before you left the house, but you are absolutely beautiful in the photos."

"Thank you, Mom," she repeated. "I must say we had a lot of fun."

"Langston has always been a nice boy."

Georgina wanted to remind Evelyn that Langston was no longer a boy, but a man. Albeit a man she'd found extremely attractive. "Yes, he is," she said.

She did not know what had occurred between her parents in Hawaii to elicit a change in her mother's temperament where she had become the woman with whom Georgina was familiar when she was a child, but she had no intention of asking either of them. She would wait and see for them to tell her where they'd gone, what they'd seen and if they planned to return soon.

"I brought you something back that I think you'll like, but you're going to have to wait for me to unpack," Evelyn said.

"You didn't have to do that, Mom."

"Yes, I did."

Georgina wasn't about to argue with her mother now that they seemed to have called a truce. "Take your time unpacking. I need to do several loads of laundry, so if you have something that needs to go in the wash, then leave it the laundry room."

Evelyn closed the newspaper. "When are you moving into your new place?"

"Tomorrow. After I leave the store I'm going directly to the house."

"Why don't you take off tomorrow and take the day to settle in?"

Georgina went completely still; she could not believe her mother was urging her to take a day off. "Who's going to help Dad?"

"I will. Things haven't changed so much that I don't know how to run the store. In fact, I'm going in for a few hours this afternoon to look after your father. There were times when he really overdid it when we were in Hawaii. I'd tried to convince him to slow down, but he wanted to hike trails to see volcanos, pineapple plantations and waterfalls. The first few days he was so sunburned that I suspected he had second degree burns, but you know he's stubborn as a mule and when he sets his mind on something it's almost impossible to get him to change it."

"You knew that, Mom, even before you married him."

Evelyn lowered her eyes. "You're right, and I suppose I have to accept what cannot be changed."

"We all have to accept what we cannot change," Georgina said in a quiet tone.

Evelyn slipped off the bench seat and approached her. If her mother's attitude had changed, so had her overall appearance. She'd gained weight, her face had filled out and the permanent frown that had settled into her features was no longer evident. It had taken more than a week and six thousand miles away from Wickham Falls for grief to release its relentless grip on Evelyn Powell.

"If you need my help setting up things, just let me know."

Georgina hugged her mother, and then pressed a kiss to her hair. "Thanks for offering, but I've been going over to the house every few days to put things away."

Evelyn wrapped her arms around Georgina's waist. "I know I haven't told you, but I am so proud of you, baby. It probably wasn't easy for you to accept that you weren't going to go to art school, yet you stepped up to help your father run the store. He never would've been able to do it without you."

She wanted to tell her mother that her husband could have done it with his wife but did not want to ruin the fragile truce forming between them. That if Evelyn had gone back to work after a period of mourning, Georgina knew she would not be planning to move into a guesthouse on the Remington property. But unlike her mother, who'd allowed herself to wallow in the past, she was looking forward.

Once she'd made the decision to open A Stitch at a Time, Georgina was forced to admit to herself that attending art school may not have been best for her future, because she would have to work for someone else. Opening a business in her hometown where she could be her own boss was heady indeed. It would become a one-woman operation and she looked forward to reconnecting with the loyal customers who'd patronized Powell's arts and crafts department.

"We're family and because of that we'll always stick together," Georgina said instead.

Evelyn eased back. "Speaking of family, I spoke to my sister yesterday and she said she's thinking about selling her house and buying a one-bedroom condo. Michelle claims she doesn't need a house with three bedrooms when she's the only one living there. She never would admit it, but I think she's trying to get rid of some of her deadbeat friends who like to hang out at her place."

"That's because Aunt Michelle is a lightning rod for the downtrodden."

"Like Sutton's father," Evelyn spat out, twisting her mouth as if she'd tasted something too salty or acidic. "I'd tried to tell her he was no good, but she refused to listen until she discovered she was pregnant, and then he took off like an antelope being chased by a cheetah."

Georgina smiled. "She's lucky because Sutton is a wonderful son."

"You're right," Evelyn agreed. "When I asked Michelle what Sutton's going to do now that he's done playing ball, she said she didn't know."

I know, Georgina thought. Sutton has sworn her to secrecy because he wanted to return to life as a private citizen with as little fanfare as possible. "You know Sutton never really liked the spotlight."

"That's because he's always been a very private person. When was the last time you spoke to him?" Evelyn asked her.

"Several weeks ago," she answered truthfully. Not only was Sutton her first cousin, but he was also the closest thing she had to an older brother. And he'd always made himself available to her whenever she needed to vent. She'd leave a message on his voice mail, and even when traveling to another city for a game he would get back to her, offering words of encouragement while volunteering to intervene on her behalf to convince his aunt to allow her to follow her dream. Georgina had declined because she didn't want to start a rift between Sutton and Evelyn.

"Did he say anything about staying in Atlanta?"

"No." She hadn't lied to her mother because Sutton did not talk about staying but leaving Atlanta.

"I'm going upstairs to get dressed, because I don't want your father to leave without me."

Georgina stared at her mother's back as she walked out of the kitchen. It would take time for her to get used to Evelyn agreeing to help her husband at the store when she'd balked at it for years. She would arbitrarily walk into Powell's to pick up something she needed, and then walk out without interacting with any of the employees, who'd gotten used to her appearing and disappearing like an apparition. Not working Sunday and Monday would free Georgina up to move in and adjust to her new home.

A shiver of excitement swept over her as she experienced a fathomless peace and satisfaction that all was right with her life.

Langston printed a copy of the town hall agenda for the first Wednesday in the month meeting that was open to the public. The mayor and deputy mayor would begin with opening remarks, followed with reports from commissioners overseeing the highway, fire department, power and light/emergency management, police and the building inspector. The meeting was scheduled to begin at 8:00 p.m. at the town hall, and usually ended before ten. Residents were always encouraged to attend and get involved in important community gatherings that directly affected them. The mayor had instituted an open-door policy where locals were welcomed to voice their concerns.

A light knock on the door garnered his attention. Swiveling on the executive chair, he saw the office manager standing in the doorway. "Yes, Sharon."

Sharon Williams walked into the office, closing the door behind her. "I need to talk to you about something that I'd like to stay between us."

Langston rose slightly, staring at the woman in her early fifties who always looked as if she'd stepped off the glossy pages of a fashion magazine. She favored suits, either with skirts or slacks, tailored blouses and her favored Ferragamo pumps. Her jewelry of a single strand of pearls and matching studs never varied from one day to the next. And no one knew the length of the brunette hair she always wore in a twist on the nape of her neck.

"Please sit down. And whatever you tell me will stay between us."

Sharon sat, nervously clasping and unclasping her fingers. She lowered hazel eyes before meeting Langston's steady gaze. "I wanted to wait until everyone left to give you notice that I will be leaving the paper in three weeks."

Langston slumped in his chair, replaying her words in his head and not realizing he'd been holding his breath until he felt restriction in his chest. "Why?"

"I'm getting married."

He was certain Sharon heard his exhalation of relief. "Congratulations!"

"Thank you, Langston. Not only am I getting married, but I will be moving to Ohio for a year."

Her mentioning Ohio reminded him why she'd informed that she was leaving the paper. He ran a hand over his face. "To say I'm shocked is putting it mildly."

Sharon smiled. "So was I when John asked me to marry him."

Langston recalled Sharon telling him that she'd reconnected with an ex-college boyfriend on Facebook and had driven to Ohio for Christmas to reunite with him. Now, five months later, she'd accepted his marriage proposal. "But why a year?"

Sharon's lids fluttered. "I tried to convince him to come here to live, but he has one more year before he can retire after thirty years of teaching."

"What aren't you telling me?" he asked when she nervously chewed her lip.

"I'd like you to approve a leave of absence for a year for me, because once John retires, we plan to move to the Falls."

Langston blew out his cheeks. Sharon was too valuable an employee to deny her request. He also planned to ask one of the part-timers if they were willing to come on full-time during Sharon's absence. "Take the year and make certain you don't forget to come back," he teased.

"Thank you, Langston. I promise we'll be back as soon as his school term ends. Meanwhile, I'm going to tell Mrs. Reilly to list my house as a rental until I return."

"Even though I'm happy for you, you have to know I don't want to see you go."

"And I really don't want to go, but I don't want to miss a chance to have my happily-ever-after."

Langston smiled despite his disappointment, because he had come to depend on Sharon from overseeing the office staff to maintaining the books. Once he assumed ownership of the paper, Sharon had become his mentor, shepherding him through every column of the biweekly for the past year, while they brainstormed how to make the periodical more reader friendly. Working as a foreign correspondent was not the same as running a newspaper, and *The Sentinel's* office manager had proved to be invaluable to and for him.

"Should I assume you don't want the staff to know you're leaving?"

"Yes, because I don't like saying goodbye. Can you tell everyone that I had to go away for a while to take care of personal business?"

"I'll tell them whatever you want, Sharon. After all, you are entitled to your privacy."

Sharon pushed to her feet. "Thank you, Langston. I'm sorry—"

"Don't you dare apologize," Langston said, interrupting her. "Do what you have to do to live your happily-ever-after." Moisture shimmered in Sharon's eyes and she raced out of the office before the tears fell.

Swiveling and leaning back in his chair, he stared out the window. Sharon talking about a happily-ever-after reminded him of the fairy tales he and Georgina had discussed. It had been more than two weeks since she'd come to his home for dinner, and he wondered if she'd finally moved into her guesthouse.

His cell phone rang and he turned to glance at the screen and smiled. It was as if thinking about Georgina had conjured her up. "Hello, princess."

"Hello, Langston. I'm calling to ask if you have plans for Sunday?"

He sat straight. "As a matter of fact, I don't. Why?"

"I'd like to invite you over to my place for dinner."

He smiled. "I'd love to come. What time and do you want me to bring anything?"

"How's three?"

"Three is okay."

"I don't want you to bring anything, Langston."

"You know we've been raised never to go to someone's house empty-handed. Didn't you bring dessert when you came to my place?"

"Yes, because you didn't mention anything about dessert. I have a fully stocked bar, and I plan to make dessert."

"Okay, Georgi. I won't bring anything." Langston knew he had to come up with something in which to celebrate her housewarming.

"I guess that settles it. I'll expect you Sunday at three."

"You've got it."

Langston ended the call. Despite what Georgina said, he had no intention of going to her home the first time without bringing something. However, he did not want to clutter his mind with the possibilities when he had to read a stack of emails for the "Sound Off" column. Once he added the column the emails began to pour in, with the proviso if printed, the complainant would remain anonymous. Although he read every one of them, there were very few that were fit to print. Complaints about abandoned cars, barking dogs or noisy neighbors were quality-of-life complaints that should've been reported to town hall.

The advantage of printing a biweekly allowed him time to read every column, the proofreader's corrections and double-check all photo captions. He was responsible for every printed word in the publication and loathed having to print corrections.

Langston read the first email and then typed it in the column's template:

We are required to bag our garbage and put it in plastic containers. Why, then, if the garbage man drops the bag and garbage spills out, can't they pick it up? The neighbors on my street have been complaining about seeing critters around looking for scraps of food.

Concerned citizens on Mayflower Drive

He decided it was a legitimate complaint and decided to include it in the column, because it was the third complaint from a different neighborhood about garbage men not picking up after themselves. Langston read another email and typed it:

I thought there was a town regulation about not owning more than three dogs per household. And if outside, they must be secured in a fenced-in yard. There is a family on Harrison Lane with five dogs and no fence. How can you allow this to go on?

Langston perused a few more emails. He had no idea when he'd created the column that it would lead to neighbors snitching on one another. However, the results were more positive than negative because it alerted town officials of incidents and infractions needed to be addressed and hopefully resolved in a reasonable amount of time. He selected one more to print:

Thank you "Sound Off." After I wrote about the unusual activity at a house on Manchester Court the sheriff's office posted a deputy in the area resulting in the arrest of the homeowner for selling drugs.

He saved the column and then forwarded it to the proofreader. Since assuming ownership of the paper, Langston scheduled staff breakfast meetings Monday mornings to discuss the tone of the upcoming issue. Unlike Eddie Miller, who always decided on the headlines and which articles would appear on the front page, Langston solicited the input of everyone on the editorial staff, reminding them they weren't a tabloid, and their focus should be on truth. It was a hometown newspaper and except for the Op-ed page, the articles steered clear of politics. As the editor, he refused to endorse any candidate, but was not opposed to them taking out ads or writing Op-eds to reach out to their constituents.

The afternoon passed slowly as he read over the article written by the reporter who'd interviewed the public school superintendent to address the issue of a potential teacher's strike because they had been working without a contract for the past three years. The teachers wanted more than a six percent salary increase over the next three years, while refusing to give up any of their hard-won benefits.

Georgina's invitation played around the fringes of his mind as he struggled to concentrate on the words filling the computer screen. Massaging his forehead with fingertips, Langston knew reviewing the article with an open mind was futile and decided to quit for the day. It was after five and everyone had gone home.

Although she had insisted he not bring anything, Langston still did not feel comfortable showing up empty-handed. He had several days in which to come up with something generic that would demonstrate his appreciation for her invitation.

It was Sunday, and after attending the early service, Georgina returned home to prepare dinner for her first and very special guest. And that was how she'd begun to think of Langston. He was special. She'd debated whether to make lamb or pork chops, and finally decided on the latter, because Langston had broiled lamb chops for her when he'd invited her to his home. But then again, she'd promised to make smothered pork chops for him.

She'd cooked for Sean, but this was different. They'd slept together, while she did not plan to sleep with Langston because it would ruin their budding friendship. She found it so easy to talk with Langston, while there were occasions when she had to struggle to make Sean open up to her. He would ask to see her, and she would drive to Beckley only to sit in his apartment waiting for him to open his mouth to say something. She'd give him fifteen minutes, then she would get into her car to reverse the trip. It would be several days before he'd call her again, and that was when she'd warn him she did not intend to drive to see him only to encounter a mute. And little did she know that he was struggling with the dilemma of how to repay his gambling debts. Although devastated when he'd asked her for money, Georgina realized Sean had done her a favor because if she'd married him or even had a child with him, her future would have been filled with not only heartache but also stress from Sean's financial irresponsibility.

Georgina had planned her menu to include a spinach salad, sautéed red cabbage with slivers of apple, a sweet potato casserole and mini apple crisps to accompany the smothered pork chops. She'd also purchased a bouquet of flowers from the local florist and votives from Powell's as a centerpiece for the table. After dusting and vacuuming and cleaning the bathroom, she felt the house was presentable for her first guest.

Georgina had settled into the guesthouse and within minutes of closing the door she believed that she'd finally come home. She felt free, freer than she ever had in her life, and chided herself for not moving out of her parents' home much sooner.

She rose at the same time each morning, lingered long enough to eat breakfast and then drove to the downtown business district to meet her father at the store. She had also continued the ritual of cooking various dishes on Sunday to last her for several days, with leftovers for lunch. It had taken Georgina less than a week to find people coming to her home to clean and vacuum when she wasn't there invasive, and informed Viviana that she wasn't going to avail herself of the housekeeping services. The owner of the B and B delivered a supply of towels and bed linens when Georgina informed her she would do her own laundry. Once she opened the door, walked in and closed it behind her, she didn't want to see evidence that someone else had been there before her.

She realized a bed-and-breakfast and hotels were run on the same model, but she wasn't spending a few days in a hotel or motel; the guesthouse had become her home—a place that had become her safe haven where she could unwind at the end of the day without interruptions or interacting with anyone.

If she'd changed, so had her mother. Evelyn had shocked her when she came into the store one afternoon and asked if she would show her the software program she had set up to keep track of the inventory. One day became two, and after a week the murmurings about seeing Evelyn in Powell's ceased altogether. When she'd asked her parents what they were doing Sunday, Bruce informed her he wanted to surprise Evelyn by driving up to Charleston after closing the store, checking in to their favorite hotel overnight and ordering room service. He appeared slightly embarrassed when he confessed that he felt as if they were newlyweds, rediscovering a passion that had been missing for far too long.

Georgina tried imagining what it would feel like to marry and even after thirty-plus years of marriage still enjoy making love with her husband. She'd convinced herself she didn't have time for a romantic liaison when it was exactly what she needed, if only to allow her to trust a man enough to believe he did not have an ulterior motive for wanting to be with her.

She opened the refrigerator and removed a bag of freshly washed spinach, a carton of mushrooms, red onion and several strips of bacon. Once she boiled an egg and let it cool, then she'd slice it for the salad along with crisp bacon.

Georgina turned on the radio on the kitchen countertop and selected a station that featured upbeat dance tunes. She'd only shared one dance with Langston, albeit a slow one. Sean had loved to dance, and he would take her to different clubs where she'd spent so many hours on the dance floor that she'd occasionally arrive home holding instead of wearing her shoes.

She lit several scented candles to offset the cooking aromas as she chopped, minced and sautéed the ingredients for dinner, stopping to shower again and change into a hot-pink sleeveless sheath dress, ending at her knee. She'd just slipped her bare feet into a pair of espadrilles with matching pink ties when the doorbell rang. Not bothering to take a last glance at her reflection in the Cheval mirror, Georgina walked out of the bedroom and to the front door.

Peering through the security eye, she saw Langston staring back at her. She opened the door and sucked in a breath at the same time her heart pumped wildly in her chest. He wore a royal blue tailored suit with a white shirt and silk tie that was the perfect match for her dress.

Her delight in seeing him again was reflected in her eyes and smile. "Welcome."

Langston extended the hand behind his back, handing her a cellophane-wrapped jade plant in a white glazed pot with black Asian lettering. "This is a little housewarming gift."

Chapter Eight

Langston knew Georgina wasn't expecting him to bring anything, but the smile softening her delicate features grew wider when she stared at the plant. "Oh, it's beautiful! Thank you so much, Langston."

"You're welcome. And may I come in?"

Georgina stepped aside. "Yes. Do please come in."

He walked into the house and glanced over Georgina's head to examine her new home. It was as charming as the woman occupying it. The ubiquitous hotel/motel vibe was missing, and in its place was a space designed for family living. A bundle of dried herbs lay on the grate in a faux fireplace and the scent of lemon from several jars of lighted candles wafted in the air. A table in the living/dining area was set for two. His gaze lingered on a vase of deep rose-pink roses and tulips.

"Lovely," he whispered. Langston shifted his gaze from the table to Georgina. "Lovely," he repeated, staring directly at her. And that she was. She had blown out her hair and pinned it up in what he recognized as a messy bun. She lowered her eyes in a demure gesture that never failed to turn him on. Everything about her was a visual feast.

"Even though I told you not to bring anything, I love the plant. Thank you so much."

"You're not going to hold it against me?" he asked.

"Of course not. I was thinking about buying a few potted plants to liven up the place. Now I'm forced to so this little guy can have some friends. What does the lettering say?"

"Love, peace and eternal happiness."

"So you also read Chinese?"

Langston laughed. "No. There was a note card attached, translating the words. This place is very nice. How many rooms do you have here?"

"Two bedrooms, galley kitchen a full bath, living/dining area and there's a king-size bed in the loft with a wall-mounted television."

Langston walked over to the window. "I've driven past the Falls House countless times and never knew these guesthouses were here." They overlooked a grassy pasture with a copse of trees and wildflowers growing in abandon.

Georgina removed the cellophane from the plant and set it on a side table. "Neither did I. Remember, the Remington kids didn't go to the public school with the rest of us, and I doubt if they had sleepovers like the rest of us."

Langston was aware that Viviana graduated from a private boarding school, while her brother Leland transferred to the high school where he hadn't made many friends. "Are your parents going to join us?"

"No. My folks are going up to Charleston later this evening to eat at their favorite restaurant." She didn't want to tell him that her parents had planned to check into a hotel for the night.

Langston smiled. "That's nice."

Georgina also smiled. "I agree. They've been acting like lovebirds since coming back from Hawaii."

"Good for them, Georgi. Just because couples have been married for a long time doesn't mean the passion gets old. My folks act like teenagers when they decide to make out in front of me and my sister."

"Aren't they embarrassed for you to see them like that?"

"Heck, no. The one time I said something to Dad, he told me in no uncertain terms that it was his house and therefore he could do anything he wanted. And when I get my own place, then, as king of my castle, I could do whatever I want. Of course, my mother differed with him because she said she didn't want her son to have a revolving door of women coming and going, because what I did in the dark was certain to come out in the light. And she said that before social media blew up."

Georgina nodded. "Your mother is right. You can have one mishap in college, and it can follow you for life."

"I'm no monk, but I've tried to be selective when it comes to who I've been involved with."

"You know there's talk about us being photographed together at the Chamber dinner-dance."

Langston's expression did not change with her mention of them possibly being linked as a couple. Jonas had mentioned it, and so had a few people he'd run into when at the supermarket. He'd been noncommittal about their so-called relationship when they'd asked if he and Georgina were dating, while he'd wanted it to become a reality.

"I know," he said truthfully. "Does that bother you?"

"No," Georgina said quickly. "I learned a long time ago not to be swayed by what folks say, because they're going to believe whatever they want regardless of how you try and convince them it's not that way."

Crossing his arms over his chest, he gave her a lengthy stare. "Are you saying you don't mind us being seen together in public?"

She laughed softly. "We were already seen together in public."

"That's not what I mean."

"I know exactly what you mean, Langston. You're asking if I would be willing to date you."

He blinked slowly. "Yes."

"Yes, but only when I have some free time."

His smile was one of supreme confidence and victory. Getting Georgina to agree to go out with him was easier than he'd anticipated. Langston did not know why but he'd expected her to turn him down.

"I promise not to get into a huff when you say you can't see me."

"Thank you, because I don't do well with bad attitudes."

His eyebrows lifted slightly. "I'll try and remember that."

"You can lose the jacket and tie, because dinner is going to be casual and relaxing," Georgina said.

Langston wanted to tell her that flowers and candles were a step above casual, but decided not to say anything. "Is there anything I can help you with?"

"You can open the wine and allow it to breathe. I've made the salad and dressing, cooked the cabbage, and the sweet potato casserole is in the oven along with apple crisps. I've seasoned and stuffed the chops, and I wanted to wait until you got here to cook them."

He shrugged off his jacket, leaving it on a chair,

loosened his tie and rolled back the cuffs on his shirt. "Do you mind if I watch you make the chops and gravy?"

"Of course not. I'm going to get you an apron, so you won't get food on your shirt."

Langston pressed his hands to his belly. He realized he'd eaten too much, but he couldn't stop himself when he had second helpings of the sweet and sour cabbage, sweet potato casserole with a topping of finely crushed sugared pecans and the fork-tender double-cut stuffed pork chops with an onion and pepper gravy that literally melted on his tongue.

"If I eat like this every day I'd end up gaining at least fifty pounds," he said, smiling across the table at Georgina. Where did you learn to cook like this?"

She smiled. "My grandmama taught me."

Langston raised his glass of rosé. "Here's to grandmothers all over the world who taught their grandbaby girls how to cook."

"Grandma Dot was old school and she told me no young woman should marry unless she knew how to cook because she didn't much believe in eating in restaurants, or husbands being able to cook."

Langston partially agreed with Georgina's grandmother. "Restaurants are necessary at times, but I personally would rather a home-cooked meal anytime to eating out. Is your mother a good cook?"

"The only thing I'm going to say is that she's better than my aunt Michelle. My grandmother gave up on them when they claimed they didn't want to be chained to a stove, which meant I was her next pupil. I loved going to my grandmother's house because whatever she made was delicious. And she was in seventh heaven whenever I asked her to teach me how to cook something I really liked. She'd sit me on a stool near the table or stove and patiently show me step by step how make perfect fried chicken or ribs."

A slight frown furrowed Langston's forehead. "She fried ribs?"

"Yes. She'd cut up ribs, wash and season them with kosher salt and lots of black and white pepper. Then she would put flour in a paper or plastic bag and coat them well. And like with chicken, she'd shake off the excess flour and fry them in oil until they're brown all over. They would take only about two to three minutes to cook. I varied the cooking method with spraying them with canola oil and oven-fry them. They come out just as crispy but with less oil."

"Wow! One of these days I want you to come over so I can watch you make them."

Nodding, Georgina smiled. "Okay."

"I'll buy the ribs from the butcher at the supermarket and have him chop them into bite-size pieces."

"What else do you plan to serve with the ribs?" she asked.

Langston searched his memory for what he'd

eaten when visiting his grandmother in South Carolina. "Potato salad and cole slaw."

Georgina's eyebrows lifted. "You're going to make potato salad?"

Langston winked at her. "You're not the only one with a grandma who could burn some pots. She did teach her grandbaby boy and girl how to cook."

Propping her elbow on the table, Georgina rested her chin on the palm of her hand. "And she taught you well, because you are quite good."

He inclined his head. "Thank you. But what I'm looking forward to is us cooking together so I can pick up some pointers from you for our next encounter."

"Are you talking about a cook-off?"

Langston winked at her again. "So I see you catch my drift," he drawled.

"Do you have any idea what you are proposing?" Georgina asked as she lowered her arm. "You have to know that Dorothea Reed won first prize for her dishes whenever she competed in the Fourth of July cook-off. Folks would always ask for her recipes, but rather than say anything she'd pretend she didn't hear them. Only her granddaughter is her recipe secret keeper."

"So it's like that, princess?"

"Yes, sweet prince. It's like that. There's a hard and fast rule that only someone related to a Powell can become management at the department store. It's the same with family recipes that have been passed down from one generation to the next. So," she said, pantomiming zipping her lips, "no can do."

Langston switched chairs, sitting next to Georgina, and took her hand, cradling it gently in his larger one before bringing it to his mouth and kissing her knuckles. "What if we were married? Would I still be exempt?"

Georgina froze. Nothing moved. Not even her eyes. It was the second time Langston referred to her marrying him. She searched his face for a hint of guile but found it impossible to read his impassive expression.

"No, you wouldn't be exempt even though that's not going to happen."

"What isn't?"

"Marriage. Several years ago I dated someone, believing I was in love with him and if he had proposed marriage I would have jumped at the opportunity to become his wife. But when I discovered he was hiding something from me I realized I had to walk away."

Langston tightened his hold on her hand. "Everyone has secrets."

She closed her eyes for several seconds. "I know that, Langston. But his secret was one that wouldn't allow me to ever trust him. And for me, trust is more important than love."

"You are preaching to the choir, babe."

A small smile trembled over her lips. "The difference between you and me is that everyone in the Falls knew about your breakup because you'd married a celebrity, while few folks in the Falls were aware that I was seeing someone."

"Was that by design?"

"Not really. He lived in Beckley and most times I'd drive down to see him."

Langston released her hand and settled back in his chair. "I found out Ayanna was cheating on me when someone at the station sent me a photo of my wife and her costar splashed across the front page of a supermarket tabloid locking lips at a Mexican resort."

"Where were you at the time?"

"Afghanistan."

Georgina gasped. She did not want to believe a woman could cheat on her husband while he'd faced impending death every second of the day. "How selfish."

"Yes and no."

She gave him an incredulous stare. "Are you saying that you gave her a pass for cheating on you?"

"No. Our relationship was very complicated. When I married Ayanna, I was more than aware of her dealing with issues of abandonment. She was twelve when her father went to the store and never came back, leaving her mother to raise her and her younger sisters on her own. When I told her about my overseas assignment we got married a week later, and our wedding night was spent with her crying and begging me not to go. I manage to convince her that it would be for less than a year, which seemed to belie some of her insecurity."

"You deceived her, Langston, because you were abroad for more than a year."

"That's where you're wrong. When I told her I was coming home, she said I could stay because she'd gotten a role in a popular Broadway play and with rehearsals and six performances a week we'd rarely get to see each other."

Georgina felt heat from embarrassment suffuse her face. She'd spoken too quickly and misjudged Langston. "I'm sorry," she said in apology. "I didn't know."

He managed what passed for a smile. "Very few people know. When I confronted her, she claimed she didn't want a divorce but there was no way I was going to remain married to a woman who didn't attempt to hide her affairs."

"Affairs?"

"Yes, Georgi. Ayanna had had several affairs during our marriage."

"But why?"

Langston pressed a fist to his mouth as he appeared to be deep in thought. "I don't know the answer to that. Some men and women need constant attention and when they don't get it at home they seek it with others."

"Do you ever hear from her?"

"She called me a couple of months before I left Washington to invite me to her wedding. But I declined and wished her the best."

"Did she marry the man with whom she was photographed in Mexico?"

"No. Her new husband is much older than she is."

Georgina wondered if Langston's ex was marrying an older man to replace her absentee father. "I hope she finds what she has been looking for in her new husband."

"So do I. Enough talk about exes. Do you have your sketches with you?"

"Yes. Why?"

"Do you mind if I see them?"

She gave him a sidelong glance. "Do you intend to grade me?"

Langston chuckled under his breath. "No. I researched the high school archives and saw old newspapers with your illustrations. I have to admit that you were very good."

Georgina stared at the tablecloth. "I'm certain I would've been a lot better if I'd gone to art school."

"That is debatable, Georgi. Some people are born with a natural talent without professional training or instruction. I've seen phenomenal work by graffiti artists who go from spray painting buildings to having their work hang in museums."

"Are you referring to Jean-Michel Basquiat?"

"Exactly. I saw an exhibition of his work in a museum and I was blown away that he used social commentary in his paintings to get his message out about colonialism and class struggles."

"Basquiat is the exception for a graffiti artist, Langston, because he did attend art school. He is what I think of as an artistic genius who was destined for fame. Unfortunately, he couldn't deal with his artistic success, and the pressures put upon him of being a black man in the white-dominated art world and he turned to drugs to cope. I admire him because he was so prolific during his short life and career, leaving the art world more than fifteen hundred drawings and around six hundred paintings."

"Imagine, Georgi, you're only twenty and meanwhile you're homeless and unemployed and you've been supporting yourself selling T-shirts and homemade post cards when suddenly a single painting sells for twenty-five thousand dollars. That's a lot for someone his age to accept."

Georgina had taken three art history courses in high school and totally immersed herself in the lives and works of artists, many of whom didn't achieve fame until after their deaths. "It is. How many artists do you know who were able to sell their work and become über wealthy during their lifetime?"

Leaning closer until their shoulders touched, Langston pressed a kiss on her hair. "Times have changed from struggling artists painting in unheated garrets while subsisting on bread, cheese and wine. And the ones who had a patron were luckier than the others. Artists today have a lot more options when they can exhibit their work at galleries or even on street corners."

"True. But as an illustrator it wasn't about becoming wealthy. I just wanted to be known as a professional artist."

"Have you thought of sketching in your spare time?" Langston questioned.

"What spare time? Right now I'm working an average of ten or more hours a day, with every other Sunday off. Then once I open my shop I will spend most of my time knitting and crocheting sale samples."

"Do you plan to open seven days a week?"

Georgina shook her head. "No way. I'm going to close Sundays and Mondays. I plan to open at ten and close at six Tuesdays through Saturdays."

"Good for you. Now, are you going to show me your sketch pad?"

"Sketch *pads*," she said, correcting him. "I have at least a half dozen pads."

"Then I'd like to see all of them."

"And what do you intend to do with them, Langston?"

"I want to observe your artistic talent before I interview you for the paper's 'Who's Who' column after you have your grand opening."

Georgina hesitated as she pondered Langston's reason for wanting to see her sketches. Pushing back her chair, she stood. "Okay. I'll get them for you."

Langston waited for Georgina to leave the kitchen before he began clearing the table. Sharing dinner with her was enlightening. It wasn't until Georgina revealed she had been involved with a man that something had communicated to him that she was a virgin. There was something in her body language that had led him to believe she hadn't had much experience with the opposite sex. She didn't shrink away whenever he touched her, but he'd detected an uneasiness in her which would not allow her to completely relax.

She'd proudly announced that she was a country girl down to the marrow in her bones, and that was what he'd found so refreshing. Georgina was open and wholesome, while not flirtatious or overly provocative, He thought of her as an enigma when she went from a bare, freckled-face woman with braided curly hair to a drop-dead gorgeous sophisticate with a subtle cover of makeup highlighting her best features. He much preferred her natural curly hair to the straightened strands. And his libido always went into overdrive whenever she wore a dress to reveal her legs. Some men liked breasts, and others were drawn to hair and hips, but for Langston it was legs.

Georgina Powell was an unpretentious small-town woman who appealed to his need to settle down and begin a life far from the glare of cameras or adoring fans who'd come to bookstores for him to sign their books. She was a reminder of how life was and could be again after the constant fear and threat of losing his life in some foreign war-torn country.

When first assigned as a foreign correspondent Langston felt as if he was on top of the world. He had recently celebrated his twenty-sixth birthday when he found himself on a jet flying to Africa and a tiny country on the continent that had gone through decades of war and genocide. He was optimistic and fearless, believing himself invincible. The first time he saw a dead body on a street that had been there so long it was bloated from the heat, he'd nearly lost the contents of his stomach. His guide laughed and told him to get used to it.

Langston never got used to seeing death and dying in all the years he remained abroad, and whenever he was granted a vacation he'd book a flight to someplace he deemed relatively safe for tourists. He'd check into hotels off the beaten track and sleep until hunger or nature forced him to get up. His facility with languages proved invaluable whenever he asked locals for places he should visit or restaurants serving the best food in town.

He fell in love with Venice, Paris, Córdoba and Granada, the Moorish cities in Spain and the tranquility of several Greek islands. The respite allowed him to regroup and refuel to return to his assignments and view them differently with the realization that it was his chosen career and he had the option of staying in or getting out.

And when his mother questioned him about not coming back to the States he told her if he had then he would not have returned. But after eight years he had decided to call it quits once he realized he was experiencing PTSD. The nightmares had kept him from a restful night's sleep. He never regretted handing in his resignation and knew he had to see a therapist to deal with the flashbacks. It took a year before he felt able to cope with his past in order to move forward.

He'd cut himself off from friends and colleagues. The exception was his sister and her family. She lived in a DC suburb and whenever he went to visit with her he was able to experience a modicum of normalcy as Uncle Lang.

Georgina returned with the sketch pads and handed them to him. "At what age did you begin drawing?"

"I had to be about six or seven."

"Do you mind if I take these home with me? I promise to give them back after I go through them."

A beat passed before she nodded. "Okay."

Langston exhaled an audible breath. At first, he thought she was going to refuse him. "I also promise not to eat or drink anything while I look at them."

"I would appreciate that even though I doubt if I'll ever do anything with them." She paused. "Are you ready for coffee and dessert?"

He set the pads on the chair at the table. "Yes, ma'am."

It wasn't until Langston drove home, changed into a pair of sweats, sat in the family room and opened the first sketch pad that he immediately recognized talent even at the age of six or seven. She'd sketched a cat asleep and stretched out on the driveway of her house. There was nothing childish or amateurish in the pencil drawing. He lost track of time as he turned page after page in each of the books, seeing the growth and confidence in the drawings as she matured.

He was transfixed with one of two little girls jumping rope. The expressions on their faces radiated joy, matching those of the ones turning the rope. Langston noticed she'd change themes from people to flowers, animals and landscapes. He went back to the ones of young children and stared at them for an interminable length of time. Then something in his head clicked when he reached for his cell phone and called his sister.

"Now, what did I do to have the honor of my favorite brother calling me?"

Langston smiled. "I'm your favorite brother, Jackie, because I'm your only brother."

"True. What's up?"

"I think I have something you should look at for your next book."

"Do you want to give me a hint?"

"No. I'm going to photograph them and send them to you. I'll text you before I send them, so Mrs. Lindemann, please don't forget to check your email." His sister claimed she had thousands of emails but loathed reading and deleting old ones.

"Now I'm really curious."

"By the way, what size sweater does Brett wear?"

"I usually go by his chest size, which is now twenty-six inches. But if you're going to buy him a pullover, then it should be at least twenty-six inches, because I always have him wear a shirt under it. And don't forget he's sensitive to wool, so it has to be acrylic."

"I forgot about that. How's Sophia?"

"Please don't talk about Miss Grown. She's all of three and trying her best to work my last nerve. I told her father that one day he's going to come home and find him with one less dependent to claim because I'm going to send her down to her grandparents to live, and you know Mama refuses to put up with a sassy girl."

"Like mother, like daughter," Langston teased. His sister did not know when to stop talking whenever Annette warned her the conversation was over, and it always ended with Jackie being grounded for weeks at a time.

"That's not funny, Langston. Just wait until you have some kids."

"And I'm willing to believe the children I hope to have will be perfect."

"Yeah, right. I hate to end this call, but Chris just walked in and I want to make certain he eats something before he goes to bed."

"Give him my best, and I'll be in touch again." His brother-in-law, assigned to the FBI's CIRG—Critical Incident Response Group, was on call 24/7.

"Love you, Lang."

"Love you, too, sis."

Langston rang off and continued to stare at the images of the children before he rose to his feet to get a camera. He had to use a wide-angle lens in which to capture the entire sketch on each page. It was close to midnight when he finally finished what he wanted to send to his sister. Jacklyn had taught school for several years before deciding she wanted to stay home with her children until her youngest was at least five. In the interim she'd fulfilled her wish to write a children's picture book. After several rejections, she finally found a publisher willing to accept it. She'd published it under a pseudonym and then bragged to him that he wasn't the only pub-lished writer in the family.

Her first two books proved to be successful, which gave her confidence to begin a series focusing on di-versity and inclusion for elementary school-age chil-dren, and Langston believed Georgina's sketches of children would be the perfect illustrations for Jack-lyn's books.

He didn't want to say anything to Georgina until after he got feedback from his sister. However, he planned to return her sketch pads in a couple of days. Hopefully, Jackie would like what she saw and would recommend the illustrator to her editor and thus fulfill Georgina's wish to become a pro-fessional artist.

Langston knew he wasn't being completely altru-istic in wanting to help Georgina realize her deferred dream. He liked her a lot and those feelings deep-ened whenever he spent time with her.

Although he'd been married, Langston hadn't been given the opportunity to feel like a husband when he was thousands of miles away from his wife. Now he craved stability that let him come home every night to his wife and children. He wanted to have family vacations and he wanted to grow old with his wife, and the biggest concern was where they would retire so they would have time to spoil their grandchildren.

To others he probably would sound naive. But if they'd witnessed what he'd experienced in his former career they would want the same.

Chapter Nine

Georgina covered her mouth with her hand to keep from screaming. Her permit to open A Stitch at a Time was approved and she could officially occupy the space in July.

After reaching for her cell phone, she punched in Sasha's number. "I got it," she said when her friend answered.

"They approved you?"

"Yes! Right now I'm doing the happy dance. I can officially open next month. I'm going to arrange for the shelving and the furniture to be delivered."

"Oh, Georgi, I'm so happy for you. I'm going to

make a batch of cupcakes and other goodies for your grand opening."

"You don't have to do that, Sasha."

"Yes, I do, so please act gracious and accept my gift."

"I can't be gracious when I'm delirious."

"I hear you, girlfriend," Sasha drawled. "And with your artistic ability, I know your shop is going to be beautiful."

"I'm going to try. You're the first one I called, so don't say anything until I go public."

"Girl, please. Your secret is safe with me. Speaking of secrets, Dwight and I were seeing each other on the down low, but now I'm ready to go public."

"I knew it! I saw the way you two were looking at each other. And you denied everything when I asked you about him."

"That was then, and this is now. I did not want to say anything because I didn't want to jinx myself. Georgi, he's wonderful. I was so turned off men after marrying that pompous, egotistical cretin that I refused to look at another one."

Georgina smiled even though Sasha couldn't see her. "It's real hard not to stare at Dwight Adams. The man's beautiful." The town's resident dentist was the epitome of tall, dark and very handsome.

Sasha laughed. "I could add a few more adjectives to describe him, but it would be too much information."

"I get the picture. I'm going to hang up now because I have to call my cousin."

"Congratulations again."

"Thanks."

Georgina had managed to calm down by the time she dialed Sutton's number. He picked up after the third ring. "Hello."

He sounded sleepy. "Did I wake you?"

"No. I was just…" His words trailed off.

"Look, Sutton. Call me when you have time." Something told Georgina she'd interrupted something she didn't need to know about.

"It's okay, Georgi. What's up?"

"My certificate of occupancy was approved, and I can officially open for business July first. I haven't told my folks because I want to know when you can come up to help out in the store."

"I can be there in a week. I closed on the condo yesterday and right now I'm staying with a friend while the movers pack up my stuff and put it in storage. I'm going to call Aunt Evelyn after I get off the phone with you and let her know I plan to stay with her until I find a house."

"Thanks, Sutton. You know I owe you."

"No, you don't. After all, we're family and that means we have to look out for one another."

"What about your mother? Does she plan to stay in Atlanta?"

"Right now, she's on the fence whether she wants

to stay or leave. She claims she's coming up for the Fourth of July celebration because it will give her a chance to reconnect with folks in the Falls."

"How long does she plan to stay?"

"I'm not sure. She claims she needs a break from her what she calls her so-call friends."

"What's wrong with them, Sutton?"

"I told her the sooner she gets rid of her entourage, the better her life will be. Once folks found out that she was my mother they began swarming around her like flies on fish guts. I told her over and over that they were using her, but Mom told me I was jealous because I didn't have any friends. What she fails to realize is that I don't need friends who are nothing more than parasites. That's where a lot of dudes go wrong because when the money runs out their homeboys find other places to park their dusty butts. I refuse to have folks laying up in my house when I'm on the road. And whenever someone asks to come over I politely give them a time to leave. I tell them I'm not running a hotel or motel, so there's no checking in."

"Wow! What do they say?"

"There's not much they can say. My house, my rules. And those who drink too much and can't drive, I arrange for a car service to take them home."

Georgina knew very few men were willing to challenge her six-four, two-hundred-thirty-five-pound cousin who could hit a baseball into the upper

deck and occasionally out of a ballpark. She knew
Sutton's aversion to having people lounging around
his house was the result of his ex-wife's constant
need to entertain her family and friends. He'd finally
had enough and filed for divorce. He gave her the
house and a generous settlement and moved into a
three-bedroom condo in a gated community.

"I'm going to let you go back to whatever you
were doing before I interrupted you," she teased him.
"Let me know when you arrive."

"FYI, I'd just finished."

"Bye, Sutton."

"Bye, Georgi."

I knew it, she thought. It was obvious he was in
bed with a woman. She hadn't known Sutton to be
a love-them-and-leave-them type of guy; however,
she knew for certain that whomever he'd been seeing
in Atlanta, wasn't going to be returning with him to
Wickham Falls. At least not until he purchased his
own home.

Georgina smiled when she realized she had to
make one more phone call. Langston had come by
Powell's a couple of days ago to return her sketch
pads and he'd picked the right time because Evelyn
had left early to prepare dinner for her husband at
home.

"I got it," she said when he answered her call. "I
can open A Stitch at a Time in early July."

"Congratulations, sweetheart. Are you ready to celebrate?"

"Not yet. I'm going to wait for my grand opening."

"Have you eaten?"

"No. Why?"

"I know I can't keep you out too late, so I'm coming over to take you to the Den. Once you're up and running, I'll take you someplace real fancy so we can celebrate on a grand scale."

Georgina wanted to tell Langston that she didn't need a fancy restaurant to commemorate what she'd planned and patiently waited for. The fact that her shop was going to become a reality was enough. However, it had been a while since she'd gone to the sports bar. The last was when Sutton had come up from Atlanta during the All Star break. When they'd walked in together he was given the rock-star treatment with fist bumps, slaps on the back and some had even asked for his autograph.

"Give me time to shower and change my clothes."

"Can you be ready in thirty minutes?"

She glanced at the clock on the microwave. It was seven-thirty. "Yes."

"I'll be there at eight."

Langston felt as if he'd been punched in the gut when Georgina opened the door. A mane of reddish-brown hair framing her face flowed over her shoulders and down her back like loose ribbons. At that moment he wanted her in his bed, the curls spilling over the pillow under her head.

He swallowed an expletive when he felt the growing bulge in his groin. "You look incredible," he said in a hoarse whisper. And she did in body-hugging black jeans and cotton black long-sleeved tee. A pair of high-heeled booties put her head level with his nose. She smiled, bringing his gaze to linger on the vibrant red color on her lips.

"Thank you. It looks as if great minds think alike because we're both wearing black."

Langston glanced down at his untucked black shirt, jeans and Doc Martens, grateful that his erection was going down. "You're right about that. By the way, I called ahead and asked Aiden to save us a table."

"You have juice like that?" she said, teasingly. Retired navy SEAL Aiden Gibson returned to Wickham Falls to assist his uncle and was now the official pit master for the popular barbecue sports bar.

"You didn't know?"

Her smile grew wider. "Should I take you with me whenever I decide to go to the Den?"

Reaching up, Langston brushed a curl away from her cheek. "Of course." He wanted so much to kiss her but knew if he did he wouldn't stop. "Let's go, Cinderella."

Georgina scooped up her wristlet with her cell

phone and key card and closed the door. "Oh, my goodness. You have your father's Mustang."

Cradling her elbow, Langston led her over to the classic car. "Dad gave it to me, and I always keep in the garage."

"It looks brand-new."

He opened the passenger-side door. "That's because I had a body shop restore the outside, and Jesse Austen took care of what was needed to be replaced under the hood."

Langston waited until Georgina was seated and belted in before rounding the car and slipping behind the wheel. He found it hard to concentrate on driving with her sitting less than a foot away. The warmth of her body, the tantalizing fragrance of her perfume and knowing she was the first woman who would accompany him to the Wolf Den made the occasion even more special.

He tapped a button on the dash, turning on the satellite radio that had replaced the one that had originally come with the car. The distinctive voice of Lionel Richie singing "Out of My Head" filled the interior of the vehicle. Langston was familiar with the song, but it was the first time he concentrated on the lyrics. It was about a man who'd lost the love of his life and couldn't get her out of his head because he'd believed their love would never die. He was tempted to change the station when he heard Georgina mouthing the words under her breath.

"You know this song?" he asked her.

She turned to meet his eyes for a brief second. "Yes. I have everything Lionel Richie has recorded, including the time when he sang with the Commodores."

"What type of music do you like?"

"I'm not partial to any genre. It doesn't matter whether it's pop, R&B, rap, hip-hop or country. I usually download music of the artists I like."

"Name some."

"Rihanna. Anthony Hamilton. Anything by Whitney Houston or Aretha Franklin. Adele and Sam Smith are my favorite British singers. And last, but certainly not the least, is Tina Turner."

Langston smiled. "I flew to Montreal to see Tina in concert during my second year in grad school for her Fiftieth Anniversary Tour, and I can honestly say it was the best live performance I've ever witnessed."

"I've seen videos of her performances, but they probably can't come close to seeing her live."

"You're right about that. I have a confession to make."

Georgina rested her hand on his, which was gripping the steering wheel. "What?"

He came to a complete stop at a four-way intersection, looking both ways for oncoming traffic before driving across the roadway. "I went to see her again three months later in London."

"No, you didn't!"

Langston's laughter floating up from his throat filled the interior of the car. "Yes, I did. I'd saved all of my tips waiting tables, so I told my professor that I had to take a few days off for some personal business, not telling him I was flying to London to see Tina because I had a mad fan crush on her."

"You really had it bad."

He shook his head. "You just don't know the half of it. I was twenty-four and young enough to be her son or even grandson, but that didn't matter because I was obsessed with her."

"How long did you stay in London?"

"Two nights. I came back so jet-lagged that it took me a while to get my circadian rhythm back to normal. I still waited tables on the weekends and the manager sent me home after I dropped one too many orders. I lied and told him that I was coming down with something and he yelled at me never to step foot in his restaurant again if I was feeling sick. I went back to my apartment and slept for sixteen hours straight and when I woke up I realized it was impossible for me to attend classes, wait tables and jaunt off on a whim to attend a concert I'd seen before."

"You were young and had the hots for Tina."

"What man wouldn't, Georgi, regardless of his age? The woman is as beautiful as she is talented." *Just like you*, he thought. Georgina's sketches, even to the untrained eye, were impressive, and he knew if she had attended art school there was no doubt she would've been a very successful illustrator. "Did you ever have a crush on a singer or movie star?"

"Yes, and too many to name. It was as if I fell in love with every leading man. He didn't have to be drop-dead gorgeous. I think it was the acting that captivated me."

"So it was the art?" Langston asked.

"Yes, because acting is an art form. But there is a distinct difference between an actor and a movie star."

"Who are some of your favorite actors?"

A beat passed. "Viola Davis, Benicio del Toro, Taraji P. Henson, Denzel Washington, Will Patton, Mahershala Ali, Meryl Streep, Angela Bassett and Michael B. Jordan to name a few."

"You really like traditional actors who are not pigeonholed into playing a particular character."

"What I like, Langston, is their versatility and their ability to morph into whatever character they've been selected to play."

He smiled. "You should've been a movie critic."

"No, Langston. I'm going to be what I always wanted to be. Someone who will be successful and in control of her own destiny."

He had wanted to tell Georgina her permit had been approved after hearing the decision while covering the meeting for the paper but decided to wait until she'd received written notification. Langston did not know why, but her joy had become his, because he realized his feelings for her surpassed friendship. Although it wasn't love yet, he knew he was falling in love with her. And when she talked about being successful, he had no doubt she would be.

Even her choice in actors and music revealed she wasn't ready to embrace the latest fads. It had taken him a while to realize he, too, was a small-town guy who, despite his worldwide travels, never felt more at home than he did in Wickham Falls. He was certain his colleagues and the friends he'd made over the years would either laugh or look at him sideways if he invited them to the Falls, while wondering what was there to lure him back into a lifestyle they probably would've said was not only boring but also predictable. But it was the predictability that Langston craved because he did not have to go to sleep or wake to the sounds of bombs and gunfire.

Georgina had spent her entire life in the Falls, while he'd spent half his life away from it. Well, he was back, and this time to stay. To stay, start over and put down roots as his father's family had done generations ago.

She had asked him whether he'd wanted to remarry and have children and he could honestly say that he did. And this time he would be there for his wife and the children he hoped to share with her.

"It's now early-June and do you think you'll be able to have your grand opening the first week in

July?" Langston asked after what had become a comfortable silence.

"I'm not sure, because a lot has to happen in a month. I must call several companies to deliver the shelving, furniture and other equipment that I've placed on order. And even before that I'm going to give the space a good cleaning."

He gave her a quick glance. "What about your stock?"

"It's in the spare bedroom. I've spent hours scanning the barcodes into a computer program to keep track of the inventory."

"Have you finished?"

"No. You'd be surprised how many shades of white there are. I began with embroidery thread and ended with bulky knit for each color."

Langston shook his head. "That definitely must be time-consuming."

"It's more like laborious but once it's done, I won't have to repeat it," Georgina said.

"Which color are you up to now?"

"Red."

"I want you to let me know when you have your grand opening because I'll make certain one of the staff reporters will be on hand to cover the event. Even before that I'd like to interview you for the 'Who's Who' column, but I won't run that until you've been open for at least a month."

"The week before I open I'd like to place an ad in

The Sentinel, offering discounts to customers who sign up for knitting, crocheting or quilting workshops."

"I'll have Randall Stone contact you for the ad. Of course, as a first-time advertiser you'll be given a generous discount with the hope that you will become a repeater in the classified section."

Reaching over, Georgina covered his right hand on the steering wheel with her left. "How much of a discount, Langston?"

He registered the teasing tone in her voice. "That all depends."

She leaned closer. "On what?"

"I don't know. You have to let me think about it."

Georgina laughed, the throaty sound echoing in the closeness of the vehicle. "You don't have to think about it, Langston. Even though I'm dating the owner of the newspaper I'm not going to ask for any special favors. After all, you are in business to make money."

"Yes, I am. But are you saying because we're dating each other that our businesses shouldn't factor into our personal relationship?"

"That's exactly what I'm saying. I want you to treat me like you would your other advertisers, and if not then you can consider this the last time I'll go out with you."

Langston did not want to believe she would stop seeing him because he'd wanted to help with her new startup. "Don't you believe in compromise, Georgi?"

"What do you think I've been doing my entire life, Langston? I've compromised not going to art school because I had to help my parents at the store. And I've compromised not having a love life because I've had to work 24/7 to help keep Powell's afloat. But that's over, because it's time for Georgina Mavis Powell to go it alone. And that means we cannot mix business with pleasure."

He'd wanted to tell her that his parents had married and worked together for more than thirty years and were now enjoying in retirement doing exactly what they wanted. And it didn't have to be any different between him and Georgina; he knew he had to understand where she was coming from, and although he'd found himself falling in love with her, he had to allow her the independence she needed to succeed or hopefully not fail.

"Okay, babe. I promise not to interfere."

Georgina gave his hand a gentle squeeze. "Thank you."

Langston wanted to tell her there was no need to thank him, because he was willing to agree to anything if it meant their continuing to date each other. Georgina was so different from the other women with whom he'd been involved that he'd almost forgotten they'd existed. There weren't so many he couldn't remember their names or faces, but when he looked back, he realized some he should have never engaged in conversation, because at the time he'd experienced a restlessness that wouldn't permit him to stay in one place for any extended length of time. And that meant he hadn't been willing to commit to a woman.

Langston was just beginning to acknowledge what had drawn him to Georgina other than her overall physical appearance. It was confidence and a resolute belief that she could accomplish whatever she wanted. She was loyal almost to a fault, because a lot of young women would've left town to seek their own fortunes rather than work for their family. She'd mentioned sacrificing a love life because she'd had to work long hours but once she became the proprietress of A Stitch at a Time she planned to close two days a week.

Yes, he thought. He was lucky because she'd agreed to see him rather than some other man and knowing this, he did not want to do anything to sabotage their fragile relationship. He drove down the road leading to the Wolf Den and maneuvered into an empty space at the rear of the restaurant. It was Saturday night, and the parking lot was nearly filled.

"It looks as if there's a full house," he said, unbuckling his belt.

"Is it always this crowded on Saturdays?" Georgina asked.

"I don't know. I usually drop by during weeknights. I try and stay away on Mondays because that's when everyone who's past and present military comes by. A lot of dudes stop by on Wednesdays for Ladies Night, with the hope that they can meet someone."

She smiled. "Don't you mean hook up?"

Langston held up both hands. "No comment."

He got out, rounded the car and helped Georgina to stand. Threading their fingers together, he led her to the front door. Other than when they'd danced together at the Chamber dinner dance, this would be the first time they would be out in public together. Langston knew being seen with the Powell girl, as many of the locals referred to her, would generate a lot of talk but it was something he was more than prepared for.

He opened the door and allowed her to precede him into the noisy, crowded sports bar. Music blared from speakers, making it almost impossible for someone to be heard unless they were standing only feet apart, while a dozen televisions were muted and tuned to various sporting events. The line at the bar was two-deep as a trio of bartenders was shaking, mixing and pouring drinks. Icy pitchers and mugs of beer lined the mahogany bar as the waitstaff shouldered their way through the throng carrying trays. Langston preferred coming to the Den for lunch when he did not have to shoulder his way through diners to find a table.

He tapped the arm of a passing waiter to get his

attention. "I reserved a table for two with Aiden. The name is Cooper."

The young man, who didn't look old enough to shave, smiled. "Come with me. Your table is in the back."

Resting his hand at the small of Georgina's back, Langston followed the waiter, stopping short when he realized they would be seated close to Dwight Adams and Sasha Manning. "What's up, Doc?"

Dwight pushed back his chair, coming to his feet. "I should be asking you the same thing, Cooper." The two men shook hands.

Sasha sprang to her feet and hugged Georgina before Langston was able to respond to Dwight. The two women were talking at the same time and he shrugged his shoulders when the dentist nodded and smiled. Langston and Sasha's brother Stephen were best friends.

Georgina turned and smiled up at him. "Langston, would you mind if we pushed the tables together so Sasha and I can sit next to each other without having to shout to be overheard."

He stared at Sasha's date. "Dwight, are you all right with us sitting together?"

"The more, the merrier," the retired army major quipped.

Langston removed the Reserved sign and he and Dwight pushed the tables together. He seated Georgina and lingered over her head. "Can I get you anything from the bar before we order?"

She met his eyes. "If I'm going to eat barbecue, then I'll have a beer."

"Wait for me, Cooper," Dwight said. "I'm also going to the bar." When they were out of earshot of the two women, Dwight asked, "Is it serious between you and Georgina?"

Langston chuckled. "A little, but definitely not as serious as it is between you and Sasha Manning."

It was Dwight's turn to laugh. "So you noticed?"

"It's as plain as the nose on your face that there's something going on between you and the town's pastry chef," Langston said, smiling.

Dwight flashed a wide grin. "I really enjoy being with her."

"Good for you."

Langston wanted to tell the dentist that he also enjoyed dating Georgina, because she was a constant reminder of the normalcy that had been missing for more than half his life. He'd convinced himself that he didn't need a woman in his life after his divorce; that he was content to remain a bachelor and not commit to any woman. Until now. Unknowingly, Georgina had changed him where he did want to remarry, become a father and raise his children in Wickham Falls, West Virginia.

Chapter Ten

"I had no idea when we spoke earlier that I'd be seeing you here with Langston," Sasha said in Georgina's ear.

She leaned closer to her friend, their shoulders touching. "He wanted to celebrate the council approving my application to open a business."

Sasha gave her a *you've got to be kidding me* look. "Do you really believe that, Georgi?"

A slight frown appeared between Georgina's eyes. "What are you talking about?"

"Open your eyes, girl. Langston Cooper will concoct any story he can to see you, and includes celebrating your new business." She held up her hand when Georgina opened her mouth to refute her. "Please let me finish." Georgina nodded. "I suspect I've had a lot more experience with men than you have, so please believe me when I say that Langston looks at you the same way Grant Richards looked at me when I met him for the first time. And that translates into I like and want what I see."

"Langston and I are friends, Sasha."

"Like Dwight and I went from friends to lovers. No one was more surprised than I was once I realized that Kiera's father was nothing like any other man I'd ever known or met. He was the first man who has allowed me to be me. My ex tried to control my career because he had to be the superstar in the family, while Dwight supports and respects the decisions I've made when it comes to the bakeshop."

"Why shouldn't he?" Georgina asked. "After all, the bakeshop is yours, and not his."

"True, Georgi. But I've been around enough successful couples to discover that men have very fragile egos, and once they realized their wives' or girlfriends' popularity begins to eclipse theirs, they do whatever they can to tear them down. My relationship with Dwight works because we don't have to professionally compete with each other."

Georgina wanted to tell Sasha that she couldn't compare and base everyone's relationship on her failed marriage. That couples broke up for myriad reasons and that envy could be added to the list of irreconcilable differences. And there was no way her enterprise would conflict with Langston's. He was a journalist and she a needle worker, which meant there would never be any competition between them.

"Are you ladies looking for company?"

Georgina's and Sasha's heads popped up at the same time, both recognizing boys with whom they'd attended school. "No!" they said in unison.

"That's enough, fellas," Langston said as he approached the table. "Go and annoy someone else."

"Now, gentlemen!" Dwight commanded when the two men lingered longer than necessary.

They saluted Dwight, backpedaled and made their way to the front of the restaurant. Georgina hid a smile. As a retired major, Dwight was the Falls' highest-ranking officer, and was well respected by the community. The divorced single father had become a very eligible bachelor; women were drawn to his lean, sable-brown sculpted face, and his large, dark, penetrating eyes and dimpled smile were mesmerizing, while his buzz-cut salt-and-pepper hair was a shocking contrast to his unlined face. Georgina shared a look with Sasha before both dissolved into hysterical laughter.

Langston set a pitcher of beer and two frosty mugs on the table, while Dwight set another pitcher filled with pop on the table with two mugs. "What's so funny?" he asked, sitting opposite Georgina.

"Those guys were our prom dates," she volunteered.

Dwight took his chair, staring across the table at Sasha. "Y'all went to prom with the MacDonald cousins?"

"It's not as if Liam and Chris Hemsworth were available to ask me," Sasha retorted.

"Or Michael B. Jordan for me," Georgina added, staring directly at Langston.

"Damn, brother Cooper," Dwight said under his breath. "I suppose we'll never be able to compete with their Hollywood heartthrobs."

Langston smiled. "I wouldn't worry too much, Major Adams. Those dudes have nothing on us."

Georgina and Sasha shared a smile. Langston was right. She wanted nothing to do with anyone who lived their life in the spotlight. But then she had to remind herself that Langston had become a celebrity in his own right with a bestselling book that had garnered the attention of Congress.

All conversation ended when a waitress approached the table to take their food order. They all agreed to order the newest item on the menu—Korean barbecue short ribs. Georgina had finished half her beer when the food arrived, and she sampled perfectly smoked chicken, fall-off-the-bone spareribs and melt-in-the-mouth brisket, but also sides of potato salad, collard greens, cole slaw and mac and cheese.

I was a carnivore tonight, she thought, touching the napkin to the corners of her mouth. Not only had she eaten more meat in one sitting than she'd had in a long time, she had also loaded up on carbs.

Georgina also knew the answer immediately when she'd asked herself why it had taken so long for her to come to the Wolf Den. She hadn't wanted to dine alone. If Sasha hadn't left the Falls, she was certain they would've hung out together. And inviting Sean to the Den had not been an option. They always dined in Beckley where he would occasionally run a tab with several restaurants, and not once had she questioned why he didn't have a credit card, or rarely carried cash.

Dwight placed his napkin next to his plate. "Now that the weather is warmer, I'm spending more time at my lake house, where the rainbow trout and small-mouth bass are literally jumping out of the water. You guys are welcome to come and hang out with us whenever you need to kick back and relax."

Georgina met Langston's eyes, wondering if Dwight was extending the invitation to him or to them. Had he thought of them as a committed couple because they'd danced together at the fund-raiser and had come to the Den together?

"I'm afraid that's not going to be possible," she said, "until later in the year."

"How much later?" Dwight questioned.

Georgina knew it was time to tell Dwight what

she'd revealed to Sasha and Langston, because once the next issue of *The Sentinel* was published, everyone in Wickham Falls would know another Powell planned to open a business in town.

"I'm going into business for myself." She told Dwight everything, watching as a smile parted his lips.

"It's about time the Falls got another businesswoman."

"I agree," Langston said.

"The invitation is still open if and when you get a break, Georgi," Dwight continued. "The same goes for you, too, Cooper."

Reaching across the table, Langston took Georgina's hand and threaded their fingers together. "We accept your rain check."

The drive from the Den back to her home was accomplished in complete silence as Georgina closed her eyes and chided herself for eating and drinking much too much. The time she'd spent with Sasha, Dwight and Langston had passed quickly and when she glanced up at the wall clock, she realized she'd lost track of time. It was close to eleven when they'd finally left the restaurant.

"We accept your rain check," Georgina said, repeating what Langston had said once they stood in the middle of her living room. "Do you realize you

gave him the impression that we are sleeping to-gether?"

Langston pushed his hands into the pockets of his jeans. "No, I didn't, babe. People see what they want to see and draw their own conclusions. If he believes we *are* sleeping together then do you want me to tell him that we're not?"

"No, but—"

"If it's no, then you have nothing to worry about, Georgi," he said, cutting her off. "Now, if you were to ask me whether I want us to sleep together, then the answer is a resounding yes."

Georgina went completely still. She hadn't ex-pected Langston to be that candid. He wanted to sleep with her, and she'd convinced herself that she did not want or need passion in her life; that becom-ing an independent business owner was enough. But even before opening the doors to A Stitch at a Time, she knew she needed more cutouts to complete the puzzle that had become her life. She'd known she wanted to live on her own and start up a business, but not falling in love, marrying and starting a fam-ily after she'd broken up with Sean, and looking back she wondered how she had allowed distrust to turn her off love.

"At least I know where you're coming from."

Langston angled his head. "And where are you coming from?"

She chewed her lip. "I like you, Langston. A lot,"

she added. "But I need time to sort out my feelings for you."

Taking two steps, he cradled her face in his hands. "And you can have all of the time you need because neither of us is going anywhere. I know where to find you and you know where to find me."

Georgina rested a hand alongside his lean jaw, went on tiptoe and brushed her mouth over his. "I promise not to run away."

"You better not," he whispered against her parted lips.

She lowered her hand. "Thank you for tonight. I really had a fun time."

Langston lowered his hands and dropped a kiss on the bridge of her nose. "It's only the first of many more to come."

He kissed her again, this time on the mouth, increasing the pressure until her lips parted, while Georgina's stomach muscles clenched and unclenched before trembling like frozen gelatin. Every nerve and muscle in her body screamed from the sensations holding her captive and reminding her of how long it had been since her self-induced celibacy. Langston kissing her, feeling the strong beating of his heart against her breasts, the pulsing between her thighs, forced her to acknowledge that she was a woman who'd denied the strong passions within her for far too long.

Pushing against his shoulder, she managed to extricate herself. "Please go, Langston, before I beg you to stay and make love to me."

He buried his face in the wealth of curls cascading down her back. "You'll never have to beg me, sweets. All you have to do is tell me what you want me to do with you."

Georgina nodded and pulled her lip between her teeth. She was unable to speak because of the pleasurable throbbing drowning her in a maelstrom that threatened to tear her apart. She'd just opened her mouth to plead with Langston to leave when he turned on his heel and walked out. Muffling a sob, she walked on shaky legs to the bedroom, fell across the bed and waited for the sensations gripping her traitorous body to ease.

She lay facedown on the quilt, eyes closed as she thought about what she'd shared with Langston since sitting next to him at the fund-raiser, and she could not believe the months had passed so quickly. He'd cooked for her, and she in turn had cooked for him, and tonight was the first time they'd appeared in public as a couple. Wickham Falls was a small town and gossip spread quickly, which meant she had to be prepared for the fallout.

Although Sasha had admitted to seeing Dwight in secret, it was apparent she was either tired of hiding or did not care who knew it, but her being seen with him at the Wolf Den spoke volumes.

Turning over, Georgina stared up at the ceiling,

wondering why it had taken her so long to come into her own. She was thirty-two, unmarried, childless, solvent and only recently had become emancipated. She'd dated a man for nearly eight months and hadn't been willing to introduce him to her parents until wearing his engagement ring. However, in her naiveté, she'd believed having a fiancé was necessary for her to ensure a modicum of independence. Combing her fingers through her hair, she held it off her face.

Circumstances beyond her control hadn't only affected her, but were also the impetus that changed her life once her father made the decision to eliminate Powell's crafts section. Rather than putting the items on sale with deep discounts, she'd boxed and stored them for what would become the next phase in the journey to control her destiny. And when she'd used Sasha as a sounding board about how stagnant her life had become, Georgina's friend confirmed what she'd already visualized.

And like Cinderella she was no longer the stepsister, existing behind the scenes, and after attending the ball and encountering her prince, she had no intention of hiding her relationship with Langston from her parents or anyone else. He was her man and she was proud of it.

Georgina smiled at her father when he rapped lightly on the door. "Good morning."

Bruce walked into the office, leaned over and kissed her cheek. "How's it going, baby girl?"

She rolled her eyes upward and wanted to remind her father that she was no longer a little girl. "Everything's good. Please sit down, Dad. I have something to tell you."

Crossing his arms over a crisp, white, short-sleeve shirt, Bruce met her eyes. "I think I know what you're going to say."

"Since when did you become a mind reader?" she teased, smiling.

Bruce took a chair opposite Georgina, leaning back and tenting his fingers. "Sutton called last night to tell me he's moving back to the Falls to help manage this place. His timing is impeccable now that you'll be opening your own shop."

Completely shocked, Georgina couldn't stop the gasp escaping her parted lips. "How did you know?"

Bruce lowered his eyes. "There are very few things that go on in this town that I don't know about." He glanced up, giving her a long, penetrating stare. "What bothers me is that you did not trust me enough to tell me what you'd planned."

She squared her shoulders while refusing to accept guilt for her actions. "What I didn't trust was for you not to attempt to sabotage my plans, Dad. If you'd made a phone call to someone at the town council to alert the landlord that I wanted the storefront I never would've been able to rent the space on Sheridan Street."

"I wouldn't have done that," Bruce said in a quiet tone.

"Wouldn't you, Dad? All you had to do was mention it to Mom and even if you did want to support me you would've caved like a deflated balloon and gone along with her."

Bruce's dark blue eyes grew hard. "That's where you're wrong, Georgina. I went along with your mother to keep peace in my home because I remember my mother constantly arguing with my father about absolutely nothing. If he said the sky was blue, then my mother would try and convince him it was lavender. It was one of the reasons why my brother and sister moved so far away. My folks were the perfect couple in public but hell-raisers behind closed doors."

Georgina never met her paternal grandparents who'd passed away within months of each other the year she'd celebrated her second birthday. They weren't the only couple in the Falls who'd attempted to conceal their volatile union. Sasha had confided to her about her parents' never-ending verbal encounters, which was why she never had sleepovers and it was the reason her brothers enlisted in the military within days of graduating high school.

And it was apparent Georgina had misjudged her father. "I'm sorry, Dad," she said in apology.

"There's no need to apologize, baby girl. I…" His words trailed off as a flush darkened his tanned face. "I need to stop calling you that. After all, you are over thirty."

She rested her hand atop his larger one. "You can call me that, but only in private." A beat passed. "Does Mom know?"

Bruce's red eyebrows flickered slightly. "Yes. I told her when we were in Hawaii. She started to go off on a tirade, but I stopped her, saying a few things I'm now ashamed to repeat. I must have gotten through to her when she finally calmed down enough for me to convince her she'd mourned Kevin long enough and it was time for her to help me run this place as she'd promised before we married."

"So that's why Mom came back so different."

"That wasn't the only reason. Getting her away from Wickham Falls was akin to shock therapy. She was trying hard to once again become the woman with whom I'd fallen in love and married. Every night was date night with intimate dinners, long walks and even longer talks. I told her she had to let you go before losing you completely. It hasn't been easy for her but she's finally seeing things my way, which, now that I look back, benefited all of us."

Georgina felt as if she had shed a lead suit with her father's disclosure. Now she didn't have to conduct her life like a covert agent, operating clandestinely to establish her business. Her parents knew and it was just a matter of time before all of Wickham Falls would know.

"Thank you, Dad, for your support."

"There's no need to thank me, Georgina. You're my daughter, my flesh and blood, and there isn't anything I wouldn't do to help you succeed. Would you mind if I invest in your new business?"

She knew her father was offering to give her money. "Yes, I would mind, because I don't need investors. Not even my father," she said, smiling.

"Promise me you'll let me know if you have a cash-flow problem."

"I will."

Georgina didn't tell him that she doubted whether she would have a cash-flow problem because she'd deposited enough money in her business's operating account to cover the rent and utilities for the next two years. She didn't plan to hire an employee and had projected she had enough inventory on hand to sustain her for at least six months, even with brisk sales. She had purchased furniture and equipment and as soon as they were delivered and set up, Georgina would alert town officials as to the date and time of her grand opening. The approved certificate of occupancy allowed her time to become operational, but now that it had become a reality, Georgina felt less anxious than she had before. It was now early June and she projected opening within a month.

"Did Sutton tell you when to expect him?"

Bruce nodded. "Sometime next weekend. Meanwhile, your mother has volunteered to work Saturdays and Sundays."

"It's good for her to get out of the house if only for a few days a week."

"That's what I told her. By the way, how much more do you have to do before you open?"

"Not too much, Dad. I emailed the vendors to confirm the date and time when I want them to deliver what I need to furnish the shop. And I'm still working on computerizing my inventory, and project completing that sometime this week."

Bruce narrowed his eyes, appearing deep in thought. "Today will be your last day working at Powell's."

Georgina's jaw dropped. "You're firing me?"

"Yes, Georgina, I am firing you, because I don't want you stressed out working here and then trying to finish what you need to open your shop. I'm going to give you a generous severance package and continue to pay your health insurance, so that's something you don't have to concern yourself with."

She didn't want to believe her father was letting her go, but she understood that he wanted her to succeed in her new venture. "Thank you, Dad."

"I should be the one thanking you," Bruce countered. "You've gone above and beyond being the good daughter when you stepped up and helped me out, and for that I'll be eternally grateful."

"Gratitude has nothing to do with it because we're family."

Bruce smiled. "You know that's what Sutton said when I thanked him for coming on board."

Georgina smiled. "I'm certain he's going to enjoy being away from the glare of cameras and reporters delving into his personal life."

"I admit he's handled being a celebrity well because he never let money or the spotlight change him like some young kids who can't handle the fame and act like a complete fool."

She wanted to tell Bruce that Sutton had confided to her that he'd seen firsthand how some of his college buddies who were signed to professional sports teams self-destructed when they either dabbled in banned substances or were embroiled in baby-mama drama, and he'd wanted none of it. Sutton had at one time stopped talking to his mother when he'd shown up unexpectedly to find his father staying with her. It was only when Michelle Reed finally cut off all communication with her son's father that Michelle and Sutton had renewed their close relationship.

"Dad, you have to know you're going to get more than normal foot traffic once the word gets out that Sutton Reed will be working at Powell's."

Bruce flashed a wide grin. "That's something I'm not going to complain about. And he's coming back at the right time. You know I usually close for the Fourth Of July celebration festival, but I'm thinking about opening one of the three days to bring folks into the store to meet Sutton."

"That's something you should give some serious thought, Dad, because you know Sutton really doesn't like being put on the spot."

Bruce paused. "He should've gotten used to that while playing ball. He was a baseball phenom and a role model for kids, and now that he's retired, he will have to contend with folks asking for autographs and if they can be photographed with him."

"Celebrity or not, he is entitled to a modicum of privacy," Georgina said in defense of her cousin. "Even though I won't be working for you, do you still want me to design the ads for the store?" she asked, changing the topic of conversation. "I promise not to charge you."

"Of course you can still design the ads, but we will have to talk about you charging me. Remember, Georgina, you're now going to be a businesswoman in your own right, and folks pay for goods and services. Although we're family you still have to be paid for what you do."

She knew her father was right. She'd come on as a full-time employee at eighteen, and in the ensuing years earned raises and bonuses commensurate with her responsibilities. Living at home was a perk because she didn't have to pay rent or buy food and was able to save an appreciable portion of her salary. The year she celebrated her twenty-fifth birthday she'd contacted a financial manager to set up a retirement account for herself, given she'd planned to work for another forty years. Little did she know at the time that she would be working for herself and that meant she would have to modify her plans.

Bruce pushed to his feet. "It's almost time to open up, so I want to give you something to think about."

Georgina stared up at him. "What is it, Dad?"

"Take time to enjoy life, because tomorrow isn't promised to any of us."

She froze. What was her father not telling her? "Is there something wrong with you?"

He nodded. "Yes. I'm a workaholic, and that's something I inherited from a long line of Powells. And because this store has earned the reputation of being the oldest family-owned business in Wickham Falls, I didn't want to lose that distinction. My fourth great-granddaddy started out selling feed to farmers before graduating to a general store and now into a department store able to compete with the big-box chains because we never cheated local folks. Even the Wolfes couldn't put us out of business when they set up a company store because we were willing to extend credit to the miners until they got paid. A few times when they'd sent their goons here to try and intimidate us, they were sent packing after we'd armed every employee with a shotgun ready to blast them to smithereens. Don't be a workaholic, baby girl. Close for vacation and holidays. And there's no need for you to work every day if you plan to have a family. I'm saying all of this because one of these days I would like to become a grandpapa."

Georgina stood up and hugged him. "I don't know about making you a grandfather in the very near future, but I do plan to open five days a week and close for the major holidays."

Bruce kissed her cheek. "That's my girl."

She sat down again once her father left the office to open the store. A smile stole its way over her features before becoming a wide grin. Georgina did not want to believe her parents knew about her future business venture but hadn't said a word to her.

It was obvious she wasn't the only one who had been hiding a secret. Leaning back in the chair, she kicked her legs in the air as if riding a bicycle. She'd planned to open A Stitch at a Time with or without her parents' approval, but knowing they wanted her to succeed filled her with an indescribable joy.

Chapter Eleven

Langston found his thoughts drifting from the agenda during the regularly scheduled Monday editorial meeting. When he'd first assumed ownership of the paper, he'd decided to switch the weekly meetings from Wednesdays to Mondays. He'd discovered the week the paper was to go to the printer, some of the reporters wanted to make last-minute changes or corrections, which had become a pet peeve for Langston.

He'd slept fitfully and once awake he found himself unable to go back to sleep. It had been the first time in more than a year since he'd had a nightmare that was a flashback of an incident he'd witnessed in Angola hours before he'd been airlifted out of the country. His therapist had warned him he would occasionally experience them because it was impossible for him to erase his memory like striking the backspace or delete key on a keyboard.

Langston forced his attention back to the reporter who was responsible for covering reporting on all school events, and that included sports. "Are you saying that the president of the teachers' union is talking about going on strike at the beginning of the next school year?"

Mitchell Garner blinked slowly behind a pair of black horn-rims. "Not really. She spoke to me off the record."

Langston's eyebrows lifted questioningly. "Off the record?" he asked. "Are you saying she wants you to mention it in the column?"

Mitchell shook his head. "No. She claims she's just giving me a heads-up of what's to come."

"If that's the case, then we won't print it," Langston said. He nodded to Randall. "You're next."

"I'm glad to report that advertising revenue is up again. I met with the developer over the weekend who's building on the Remington property, and he says he wants us to run a series of full- and half-page ads beginning with the August issue advertising the newly constructed homes." A smattering of applause followed his announcement.

"Good work," Langston said, smiling and complimenting the advertising salesman. "I…" His words trailed off when his cell phone vibrated; he glanced at the screen. His sister was calling him. He found it odd that Jacklyn would call him during the day when they usually spoke to each other in the evening. Standing, he picked up the phone. "Please hold on." He glanced at those sitting at the table in the conference room staring back at him. "Excuse me, but I have to take this call. What's wrong, Jackie?" he asked as he walked into his office and shut the door behind him.

"There's nothing wrong, Lang."

"If there's nothing wrong, then why are you calling me in the middle of the day?"

"I didn't think I needed permission to call my brother before the sun went down."

He smiled for the first time since answering the phone. "You don't. But you're so regimented that I thought something had happened."

"It's called being disciplined, Lang. And if I wasn't then I would never get anything done with two young children and a husband who has a go-bag sitting at the door because he never knows when he's going to be called to leave at a moment's notice. Now, back to why I called you, and I promise not to take up too much of your time. Remember the sketches you sent me?"

"Of course."

"Well, after looking them over I decided to write

another book based on the drawings of kids. I submitted it to my agent, who in turn sent it to my editor. I'm telling you all of this to let you know they want to publish the book with the illustrations. But first you have to let me know who the illustrator is so the publisher can contact him or her to offer them a contract."

Langston sat down heavily in his chair. He knew Jacklyn's contract with her publisher had given her the option of choosing the illustrator for her best-selling series of children's books based on diversity; however, when he'd downloaded photos of Georgina's sketches of children, he had deliberately not revealed the identity of the artist.

"Are you sitting down, Jackie?"

"Yes. Why?"

"She's someone you are familiar with."

"Langston Wayne Cooper, I don't have time to play guessing games with you. Just tell me her name!"

"Damn, sis. Why did you have to go and blurt out my whole government name?"

"I did it to get your attention."

"Well, you did. The artist is Georgina Powell." There was complete silence for nearly thirty seconds. "Jackie, are you still there?"

"Yes, I'm here. I… I'm just trying to process that someone I'd graduated with is going to be the illustrator for one of my books."

Langston wanted to warn his sister not to get ahead of herself, because Georgina was totally unaware that he'd sent her sketches to Jackie. "You're going to have to wait to celebrate because Georgi doesn't know I sent you her drawings."

"What! Have you gone and lost your mind, Langston? When you sent me the sketches the only thing you said was that they belonged to a friend and that you wanted me to look at them for some of my books. And now you tell me that Georgi has no idea her illustrations will appear in a book? I don't know what's going on between you and the Powell girl, but whatever it is I want and need you to convince her that I want those illustrations and that I'm going to tell my agent to get as much money for her that the publisher is willing to part with."

Langston knew his sister was angry, and he didn't blame her; he'd always been able to deal with Jacklyn's quick temper. He didn't know Georgina well enough to gauge her reaction to the news that she was about to become a professional illustrator. "I had no idea you were going to send them to your agent and editor. And that means I'm going to have to talk to her."

"Do more than talk, brother, because I want those illustrations. Better yet, why don't you convince her to come to DC so *we* can talk? Georgi and I weren't close like her and Sasha Manning, but we did speak to each other. After you talk to her I'd like you to give her my number. If she's going to turn me down, then I want to hear it directly from her."

Langston glanced at the clock on his desk. It was time he got back to his meeting. "I'll be in touch, Jackie."

"You do that, brother love."

"Yeah, right. Now it's brother love." He ended the call not giving her chance to come back at him. He loved his sister unconditionally, but there were times when she irked him because either it had to be her way or no way, and he didn't envy his brother-in-law who appeared unfazed by his wife's mercurial moods, claiming most artists were temperamental. Not only was Jacklyn an incredibly talented teacher and writer, but she was a whiz when it came to financial investments. So much so, that Langston had trusted her to handle his finances. She'd set up an account for his retirement and another that he could access without incurring a penalty for early withdrawals. It was this account he'd used for midyear and Christmas bonuses for the newspaper's staff.

"Sorry about that," he said in apology when he walked back into the conference room.

The meeting continued when the reporter who covered all social and civic events gave her report. Once everyone with a byline finished, the session adjourned minutes before a delivery person from Ruthie's arrived with lunch. Langston had begun the practice of ordering lunch for everyone after the editorial meeting and it was the least he could do for a staff who had been willing to take pay cuts while he worked tirelessly to ensure the paper's viability. After the first six months he was able to restore some of the salaries, and he projected with the increasing revenue he hoped to offer more raises and larger bonuses.

The most important thing on his mind now wasn't the newspaper, but how to tell Georgina that she could possibly become a professional illustrator with the publication of his sister's next children's book.

The ringing of the phone on the bedside table penetrated Georgina's much-needed sleep. She'd spent every waking hour preparing for the grand opening. She'd completed scanning and cataloging every piece of merchandise, including thimbles and sewing needles.

There had been a delay in shipping the reception-area furniture, and delivery and installation of the shelving was also pushed back several weeks. The warehouse foreman hadn't been able to give her a tentative date; he promised to call her the first week in July to give her an update. She'd given up projecting a date when she would open and had resigned herself that it would eventually happen.

Opening one eye, she reached for the phone and tapped the phone app. "Good morning, Langston."

"It's afternoon, babe."

She sat up. "I decided to lie down, but I must have fallen asleep."

"Are you all right?"

"Yes. Why?"

"What are you doing sleeping in the middle of the afternoon? And, where are you?"

Reaching around her, Georgina adjusted the pillows cradling her shoulders. "I'm home."

"Why aren't you at the store?"

"I no longer work at Powell's because my father fired me yesterday."

"What!"

Covering her mouth, she smothered a laugh. Georgina was surprised that the news hadn't gotten out that she no longer worked at the department store. The employees probably thought either she'd taken vacation time or wasn't feeling well.

"He let me go so that I could concentrate on what I need to do to open my shop."

"I thought the two of you had a falling out!"

Georgina smiled. "That's not going to happen. Dad and I don't agree on everything, but there's no way he's going to turn his back on me. Now, sweet prince, why are you calling me in the middle of the day?"

"I have something to tell you, but I'd rather say it in person."

She paused. There was something in Langston's

voice that made the hair on the back of her neck stand up. "Is it something that's going to upset me?"

"I don't believe it will."

"If that's the case, then why don't you tell me now?"

"It's somewhat of a surprise."

"Can't you give me a hint, Langston?"

"No, then it wouldn't be a surprise. Can you come to my place tonight?"

"I suppose I can. What time do you want me to be there?"

"Seven. We can have dinner and then watch a movie."

Georgina smiled. "I like the sound of that."

"I'll see you later."

She hung up, wondering what sort of surprise Langston was planning. She knew she'd shocked him once she told him she'd been fired. When her father had decided to let her go it was the best thing that could've happened to her, because it freed her up to do whatever she wanted and needed to do for the eventual opening of A Stitch at a Time.

She had gone online to order framed prints of anything resembling needlecrafts, and she'd also contacted someone to paint the name of the shop on the plate-glass window. Meanwhile, she'd designed her own logo for letterhead and note pads. It had taken several hours before she'd decided on a square with underground railroad quilt codes. The codes were special for her because she'd inherited a collection of quilts from her third great-grandmother who'd been a conductor in assisting blacks escaping the bonds of slavery to seek freedom in the North and Canada. The logo was the perfect complement for the shop's name because there was a time when quilts were made a stitch at a time; it was a process she enjoyed more than machine stitching because she'd found it more relaxing.

Georgina decided to stay in bed because she'd been up most of the night printing sticker prices for every item in the inventory. The task was time-consuming and laborious, but when she'd finally finished the sun had come to signal the beginning of a new day. Blurry-eyed and stiff-limbed, she'd managed to shower without falling over from sheer exhaustion and had stumbled to the bed and fallen asleep within seconds of her head touching the pillow. She set the alarm on her phone for five, turned on her side and went back to sleep.

Langston came down off the porch when Georgina pulled into the driveway and came to a stop alongside his Jeep Wrangler. He opened the driver's-side door, waited for her to scoop a decorative bag off the console and then helped her down.

He resisted the urge to kiss her when he spied a couple coming out of their house. He waved to them, and both returned his wave. Mr. and Mrs. Daniel

Howard sat on their porch every night regardless of the weather, listening to their favorite radio station. His house and the Howards' were the only two homes in the cul-de-sac. They'd moved to the Falls nearly twenty years ago and normally kept to themselves. The rumors they were in the witness protection program proved unfounded when the truth was revealed that they'd sued a hospital for the wrongful death of Mrs. Howard's identical twin sister.

"You look incredible." And she did, in a pair of white cropped slacks, a zebra-striped off-the-shoulder top and black flats. She'd styled her curly hair in a single braid.

Georgina smiled up at him. "Thank you. I brought red and white wine."

He took the bag from her grasp and led her around to the rear of the house. "Do you mind if we eat outdoors tonight?"

"Of course not. The weather's perfect for a cookout."

Langston had made it a practice to cook outdoors during the warmer weather. After his parents installed the outdoor kitchen and gazebo, they'd enclosed the rear of the property with a fence high enough to ensure a degree of privacy from their nearest neighbors. He'd lit a few citronella candles to warn off insects and covered platters with mesh domes to keep them off the food.

He seated Georgina on a cushioned chaise. "I decided to go with seafood tonight after all of the meat we ate the other night."

"Good, because I'd truly earned my carnivore badge that night."

Cradling the back of her head, he leaned down and brushed a kiss over her mouth. "I didn't want to do that with someone eyeballing us."

Georgina stared at him, completely confused. "You invite me to your home, and now you're concerned whether someone will see you kissing me?"

Langston hunkered down in front of her. "I don't have a problem with folks seeing you here, but what I'm not comfortable with is public displays of affection. I know what it is to be the object of gossip because my ex flaunted her affair for the world to see. I refuse to put you in a category where folks talk about my putting you in a compromising position. In other words, what goes on behind the doors and fence of the Cooper house, stays here."

Cradling his face between her hands, Georgina leaned closer and pressed her mouth to his. "Thank you."

He smiled. "There's no need to thank me, Georgi. There's only one thing I want from you."

She felt her heart stop and then start up again in a rapid beating that made her feel slightly light-headed. "What is it?" The query had come out in a breathless whisper.

"Please don't change."

Georgina was certain Langston had registered her exhalation of relief. She didn't know why, but she'd expected him to ask her to sleep with him. It's not that she didn't want to share his bed, but it had to be by mutual agreement.

"I won't because I can't. What you see is what you get."

"I happen to like what I see, babe."

"Ditto," she countered.

There wasn't anything about Langston Cooper that she did not like. Aside from his overall masculine attractiveness, he was intelligent, artistic and modest. He'd won awards as a war correspondent, become a *New York Times* bestselling author, survived long, grueling sessions when appearing before a congressional committee and had managed to put to rest the gossip surrounding his failed marriage once he refused to vilify his estranged wife for her infidelity.

"I'm going to feed you first before I let you in on my secret."

"Do you need help?"

Langston ran a finger down the length of her nose before standing straight. "No. Just sit and relax. I've prepped everything. The only thing that's left is heating up the grill."

Georgina stared at his retreating back as he walked to the six-burner grill. The Coopers, like so many in their enclave with their homes set on quarter-acre lots, had installed outdoor kitchens. Cooking outside offset heating up their homes during the summer months and provided space to entertain friends and family. There had been a time when her mother had become the consummate socialite when she hosted meet-and-greets for candidates running for public office, or for a contingent of women's groups seeking for more representation in local government. Everyone waited for her period of mourning to end where she would emerge once again as the Falls' social doyenne, but they gave up once one year stretched into two and beyond, and Georgina doubted if Evelyn would return to the life before losing Kevin, because she seemed very content working in the store where she greeted customers and employees alike with a kind word and friendly smile. Bruce had gotten his wife back, and she had gotten her mother back.

Smiling, she closed her eyes and let her senses take over. Georgina found the scent of citronella mingling with those of newly opened blood-red roses intoxicating. The distinctive hoot of an owl could be heard over the twittering of birds hopping nimbly from branch to branch. It was dusk, her favorite time of the day, when everything appeared to slow down in preparation for nightfall and sleep. In-ground solar lights came on, illuminating the area in a soft golden glow.

Her thoughts drifted off when she tried to imagine what it would feel like if she and Langston were married and they ended their day together relaxing outdoors. And starting a family would not negatively affect her business, because she would set up a nursery in an area of the shop's storeroom with a monitor to keep an eye on her son or daughter.

"Georgi, it's time to eat."

She opened her eyes and placed her hand on Langston's outstretched palm. Pinpoints of heat stung her cheeks when she realized where her thoughts had gone. She'd fantasized being married to Langston and having his child when they'd admitted to liking each other. And liking was a far cry from love or even falling in love. But then she had to ask herself if she was falling in love with him and she had to admit she was.

Georgina had believed herself in love with Sean yet when she compared her feelings for him to Langston, they did not come close. It wasn't until she walked away from him that she was forced to acknowledge that their relationship was wholly physical. He was the first man with whom she'd slept and had confused sex for love.

"Something smells wonderful."

"I hope you'll like what I made."

Resting a hand at her waist, Langston directed her to the gazebo where he'd set a table for two, along with a bottle of champagne in an ice bucket and a couple of flutes. A trio of lights hung from the ceiling. Mouth-watering aromas wafted from a large platter with grilled fish and vegetables.

Smiling, she sat on a cushioned bench seat. "You're incredible. I think I'm going to keep you." He'd grilled shrimp, lobster tails, scallops and pinwheels of sole stuffed with crabmeat.

Langston sat opposite her, filled the flutes with champagne and handed one to her. "It's not going to be that easy to get rid of me."

She took the flute. "What are we celebrating?"

He stared at her over the rim of his glass. "The possibility of you becoming a professional illustrator."

Georgina looked at him as if he had taken leave of his senses. "What are you talking about?" She listened in complete shock when he revealed he'd sent her sketches to his sister, who'd given up teaching to become a children's book writer.

"Jackie wrote a picture book based on some of your sketches and sold it to her publisher. What she needs is your approval to publish the book with your illustrations. She publishes under a pseudonym as Laila Lucien."

Georgina hadn't realized her hands were shaking when she put the flute to her mouth and drained it. She was familiar with the pseudonym because the author's books had won several awards, and it was obvious Langston wasn't the only award-winning writer in his family.

"Why, Langston? Why did you do it?"

"I'm surprised you've asked me that. Don't you know I'm falling in love with you, and I would do whatever I can to make you happy?"

She held out her flute for him to refill it. Everything was coming at her so fast that she found it hard to process any of it. Langston had just admitted to being in love with her while his sister wanted her as an illustrator for one of her books.

A weak smile trembled over her lips and she forced herself not to break down completely as twin emotions of shock and wonder eddied through her. "I don't know what to say. I… I had no idea you loved me."

"Remember when I asked you if you believed you were unworthy for a man to care about you and you said *of course not*? Which is it, Georgi?"

She lowered her eyes. "I am worthy."

"Yes, you are. And one of these days I'm going to prove to you just how worthy you are."

"I have a confession to make," Georgina said after a pregnant pause."

Langston gave her a lengthy stare. "What is it?"

"I love you, too." Admitting to him what lay in her heart felt as if a weight had been lifted, that what she'd been fighting for weeks had ended in a glorious victory.

Rising, Langston rounded the table and kissed her, this kiss so different from the others they'd exchanged. It was as gentle as a caress, and she was overcome with emotion she felt like crying tears of joy. He ended the kiss and retook his seat, smiling.

"To be continued," he promised. "After we eat, I'm going to call my sister because she wants to talk to you."

Georgina picked up a pair of tongs to serve herself, eating but not really tasting any of the deliciously prepared fish and vegetables, but found herself drinking more wine than she normally would under another set of circumstances.

Everything was falling into place and all was right in her world. She had always wanted to become a professional illustrator and that could possibly happen if she agreed to the terms in a publishing contract, and she'd fallen in love with a man who hadn't asked anything from her, unlike other men she'd met or known.

"What are you thinking about?" Langston asked, when the corners of her mouth lifted in a smile.

"I do love you, Langston. You're so different from other men I've known that there are times when I'm just waiting for the other proverbial shoe to drop where I'll stop trusting you."

Langston speared a shrimp but halted putting it into his mouth. "I will never cheat on you."

Georgina doubted whether he would cheat on her

because of what he'd gone through with his ex-wife. "I'm not referring to infidelity."

A slight frown furrowed his smooth forehead. "If it's not infidelity, then what is it?"

"Money."

Langston gave her a look mirroring his disbelief. "Money?"

"Yes."

He listened, appearing stunned by her revelation that boys wanted to date her because they saw her as a good catch, and her last serious boyfriend had asked her for money to cover his gambling debts. "I don't need your money, Georgi. Not today, tomorrow or fifty years from now."

A beat passed as they stared at each other, and then she said, "I believe you."

Langston smiled. "Now that we've settled that, I'm going to call my sister so we can FaceTime her." He came around to sit next to Georgina. Picking up his phone, he tapped Jacklyn's number. "Hey, Jackie. I'm here with Georgina," he said when her face appeared on the screen.

"Hi, Georgi. Long time no see."

"I could say the same about you. Your brother told me that you're now an award-winning children's book writer." She had to admit time had been more than kind to the woman with whom she'd shared several classes in high school. Jacklyn had left the Falls to attend Howard University while she had stayed behind in their hometown. Shoulder-length twists framed a dark brown complexion that glowed with good health.

"That's something I don't advertise as Jacklyn Lindemann. As the wife of an FBI special agent I like to keep a low profile."

Georgina nodded. "I understand. It appears as if your brother went behind my back to send you some of my sketches."

Jacklyn laughed. "That he did. If he'd told you in advance what he was going to do would you have agreed to it?"

Her question gave Georgina pause. "I doubt it," she said truthfully. "I'd given up the dream of becoming a professional illustrator a long time ago."

"Well, get ready for your dream to become a reality because I love your sketches and I'd like for you to come to Alexandria whenever you have time to meet with me and my agent to go over some legal work."

"Can't it be done with a conference call?"

"No, because my agent is paranoid about talking on the phone. She once represented a client whose phone was bugged by the government because he apparently was involved with some shady business, and that meant they were taping her conversations with him, as well. When they gathered enough evidence he was charged with trafficking in illegal substances."

Suddenly, Georgina felt as if she was caught in

the crosshairs of a situation with people who used fake names and were suspicious of conducting business on the telephone. "How long do you think it will take?" Although Alexandria, a suburb of Washington, DC, wasn't far from Wickham Falls, Georgina did not want to be away that long because she wanted to be available once she got the call confirming the furniture delivery.

"Probably no more than a day. Why don't you and Lang come during the July Fourth holiday weekend? Amelia can take the train down from New York and stay over, and that way we can discuss business without y'all having to rush back."

When Jacklyn mentioned their staying over at her house, she wondered what Langston had told his sister about their relationship. Even though they hadn't slept together she wanted to be an adult if they were assigned the same bedroom in his sister's house. "I'm free, but you'll have to ask your brother." She smiled when Langston elbowed her gently in the ribs.

"When do you need us to be there?" he asked his sister.

"Either Friday night or Saturday morning. As soon as I get off the phone with you, I'm going to send Amelia a text to let her know you're going to be in town. Once she confirms I'll text you back to let you know what day we're going to meet."

"That sounds good, Jackie."

"Thanks, Georgi, for agreeing to let me use your

illustrations for my new series. I know it's going to do well, and that means you'll become my personal Tomie dePaola."

Georgina laughed. Tomie dePaola had written and illustrated more than two hundred fifty books, many she'd read as a child. "Tomie is definitely an icon."

Jacklyn waved. "I'm going to hang up now and contact Amelia. Lang, look for my text so we can plan the weekend accordingly."

"Okay, sis."

Georgina waited for him to set down the phone and then asked, "What did you tell your sister about us?"

"I didn't tell her anything other than I saw your sketches and thought she should look at them. Why?"

"Okay."

"Just okay, Georgi?"

"Yes."

He shifted closer to her, close enough for her to feel his breath in her ear. "You know I don't like public displays of affection and I'm also not one to kiss and tell. What goes on between you and me is not a topic for discussion. Not even with my family."

Georgina closed her eyes and rested her head on his shoulder. It would take her a while before she would get used to a man mature enough to know who he was and what he wanted. "I like your surprise," she said after a comfortable silence.

"I'm glad you did."

"How will I ever thank you, Langston?"

He chuckled softly. "I'm sure I'll think of something that we both like."

"I'm going to have to hang out here a little longer because I exceeded my two-drink limit." The bubbly wine had temporarily dulled her reflexes and she didn't trust herself to get behind the wheel.

Langston kissed her hair. "You can spend the night if you want. I can put you up in one of the spare bedrooms."

"If that's the case, then I'm going to need a toothbrush and a T-shirt."

"Your wish is my command, princess."

Georgina shifted until their mouths were only inches apart. At that moment not only did she want him to kiss her again but also to make love to her. "I'm also going to need you to give me a raincheck for that movie."

He nuzzled her ear. "Consider it done. What else do you need from me?"

She knew if she didn't say it, then the time would pass, and she would be left chiding herself for being a coward. "I want you to make love to me." The words were out, and she couldn't retract them. Since becoming involved with Langston she'd found herself fantasizing about his making love to her.

Langston blinked slowly. "Is that what you really want, babe?"

"Yes. And please don't make me beg you."

"That's something I don't ever want you to do. And you have no idea how long I've waited for you to say those words."

"How long?"

"Too long. I have to clean up out here, and then I'm going to show you just how much I've come to love you."

Chapter Twelve

Langston didn't want to believe his fantasy was going to become a reality when he reentered the bedroom to find Georgina in his bed. However, he knew making love to her tonight was not a possibility because she'd fallen asleep waiting for him while he'd extinguished candles and put away the remains of their dinner. Light from a bedside lamp provided enough illumination for him to observe the rhythmic rise and fall of firm breasts under his T-shirt. He smiled. It was apparent the clothes she'd chosen to wear had artfully concealed a lithe, lush, very feminine body. She had loosened the braid and a profusion of wayward curls covered her pillow. To say she was sexy was an understatement.

He walked into the bathroom to brush his teeth and when he returned to the bedroom Georgina rolled over on her side, facing away from him. Slipping into bed next to her, Langston reached over and turned off the lamp, plunging the room into darkness. Georgina stirred slightly when he pressed his chest to her back, but did not wake up. Resting an arm over her hip, he closed his eyes and sank into a deep, dreamless slumber.

Georgina woke with a start, eyelids fluttering as she tried focusing on her surroundings. Suddenly, she remembered she was in Langston's bed. She tried sitting up, but the arm on her midsection weighed her down.

"Stop wiggling, babe."

"What time is it?"

"Why?"

"Because I need to know." Georgina was so disoriented that she felt like Alice in Wonderland who'd fallen down the rabbit hole."

Langston removed his arm and reached over to peer at his cell phone. "It's 11:14."

She sighed audibly. "I thought it was much later."

He kissed the nape of her neck. "What's the matter, Cinderella? Do you still have to get home before midnight?" he teased.

Georgina laughed as she shifted into a more comfortable position. "I've transitioned from Cinderella to Sleeping Beauty. I can't believe I drank that champagne."

"You only had two glasses because you didn't finish the third one."

"That's where I went wrong because I never should've accepted the third one. Shame on you, Langston Cooper, for trying to get me tipsy so you could take advantage of me."

"I would never take advantage of you, babe. And I would never do anything to you that you don't want me to do." His hand splayed over her flat belly moved lower to the waistband of her panties, and still lower to cover her mound under the lacy fabric. "Does it bother you if I do this?"

Georgina sucked in her breath. "No," she gasped.

His hand slipped under the waistband and it was flesh against flesh. "What about this?"

She closed her eyes and liquid fire shot through her. "That feels so good."

Langston buried his face in her soft, scented hair, breathing a kiss on the fragrant curls. His mouth moved slowly to the side of her neck, pressing a kiss to the velvety flesh. Using a minimum of effort, he turned her over on her back and moved lower, down to her throat, tasting the sweetness of her skin. Even in the dark, she was a visual feast. He continued his oral exploration when he divested her of the T-shirt and his mouth closed over her breast, suckling until the areola pebbled like tiny seeds. His hands were as busy as his mouth when he relieved her of the scrap of lace that made up her panties.

The moans coming from Georgina's throat were Langston's undoing. He'd hardened so quickly that it made him light-headed. He knew he had to slow down or his making love with her would be over before it began. Taking deep breaths, he flicked his tongue over her nipples, worshipping the flesh covering her perfectly formed full breasts. Langston loved her smell, the way she tasted, and now that he'd openly acknowledged he was in love with her he wanted her to be the last woman in his life.

He wanted to taste every inch of Georgina's fragrant body, but wasn't certain whether she had experienced a full range of lovemaking. She may have had sexual intercourse, but he wondered if she'd ever been made love to. And that was what he wanted to do—make love to her. His touch and kisses became bolder as his tongue dipped into the indentation of her belly button. Attuned to the changes in her breathing, the slight movement of her body, Langston took his time giving and receiving pleasure. Her hands went to his head when he buried his face between her thighs to inhale her distinctive feminine warmth and scent.

Her fingernails bit into his scalp as her hips lifted. "Easy, baby," he crooned softly. "Let me make you feel good." She tried to sit up, but his right hand splayed over her belly stopped her. "Relax, darling. I'm not going to hurt you."

Georgina wanted to tell Langston there was no way she could relax when she was drowning in erotic sensations that heated the blood coursing through her veins, taking her to a place where she had never been. She'd had only one man by whom to judge Langston's lovemaking, and there was no comparison. This was no frantic coupling, but a slow, measured seduction that had her craving his caress, his kiss. Everywhere he touched her ignited a burning passion that grew hotter and hotter until she found herself gasping in the sweetest agony.

The barrier she had erected after she had ended her relationship with Sean was swept away with the onslaught of desire that weakened her defenses, and she opened her heart to welcome the pleasure that had eluded her for years.

He lessened his sensual assault on her flesh when he reached into the drawer of the bedside table and removed a condom. It took only seconds for him to protect her from an unplanned pregnancy. Currently having a baby was certain to short-circuit all her plans.

"It's all right, sweetheart," Langston whispered in her ear, when he positioned his erection at the entrance of her femininity. She grew stiff when he pushed against her long-celibate flesh. "Breathe, baby. Just breathe," he crooned over and over.

Georgina felt the increasing pressure as he finally eased his sex into her body, which flamed with fire one minute, and then she trembled uncontrollably from cold the next. The hot and cold sensations continued until the heat won and love flowed through her like thick, warm, sweet honey. Her arms went around Langston's strong neck, holding him where they'd become heart to heart, flesh to flesh and soul to soul. Establishing a rhythm as if they'd choreographed their dance of desire, she discovered a pleasure that sent shivers of delight up and down her spine. He had promised to make her feel good, and she did.

She felt the contractions. They began slowly, increasing and growing stronger until she was mindless with an ecstasy that shattered her into a million little particles. Georgina screamed! Once, twice, and then lost count as the orgasms kept coming, overlapping one another. She dissolved into an abyss of satisfaction that swallowed her whole. She was too caught up in her own whirling sensations of fulfillment to register the low growl exploding from Langston as they climaxed simultaneously. They lay together, savoring the feeling that made them one with the other.

Georgina moaned in protest when Langston pulled out. Turning over on her side, she lay drowning in a maelstrom of lingering passion that lulled her into a sated sleep reserved for lovers. She was unaware when he had left the bed to discard the condom, or when he returned to the bed, eased her against his body and joined her in a slumber that was a long time coming.

Georgina opened her eyes, her breathing faltering. The slight ache between her legs and the hard body pressed to her back silently communicated she wasn't the same woman who'd awoken the day before.

"Good morning, baby."

"How did you know I was awake?" she asked, because she hadn't moved. A sliver of light came through the drawn drapes.

Langston pressed a kiss to her bare shoulder. "Your breathing changed."

She smiled. "How long have you been awake?"

Rising on an elbow, Langston leaned over and brushed a wealth of curls off her cheek. "Not too long. I was waiting for you to wake up to ask what you'd like for breakfast."

Turning over she smiled at him. The emerging stubble on his lean face only enhanced his overall masculinity. "Surprise me."

"Continental or American?"

"American of course." When given the choice Georgina always preferred a traditional Southern breakfast with bacon, eggs, grits and biscuits, but usually waited for the weekends when she did not have to work Sundays. Now that she no longer worked at Powell's she had a lot more options when it came to her meals. "I need to shower before I eat."

The words were barely off her tongue when Langston scooped her up as if she weighed no more than a small child. "We'll shower together so I can wash your back."

She buried her face against the column of his neck, pressing a kiss under his ear. "Be careful, because I spoil easily."

"Princesses are born to be spoiled. And the next time we have a sleepover, don't forget to bring a few changes of clothes."

"You do the same whenever you stay over at my place."

"It's like that?"

"Yes, Langston, it's like that."

"What do you think about us living together? You give up the guesthouse and move in here with me."

Georgina wanted to scream at him because they'd made love only once and he was ready to shack up with her. Well, that wasn't happening because she'd just moved out of her parents' home and she wasn't about to give up her newfound freedom to cohabitate with a man.

"I can't, Langston."

He stopped at the entrance to the bathroom and met her eyes. "You can't or you won't?"

"Both. I wasn't raised to shack up with a man and

don't forget that I just moved out from my parents' house and it feels good not to answer to anyone but myself as to my whereabouts."

His lids lowered as a wry smile twisted his mouth. "Point taken. Forgive me for bringing it up."

"There's nothing to forgive. Something must have prompted to you ask, so I want you to feel free to say whatever is on your mind."

Georgina felt something had changed between them when Langston set her on her feet. The intimacy they'd shared had vanished quickly, and in its place was a wariness that communicated to her that her lover wasn't happy with her response. What he needed to understand was that she did not move out of her parents' home just to move into a man's. The days when women moved out of their father's house and into their husband's were over.

Perhaps if Langston had become involved with her when he first returned to the Falls she would've jumped at his offer, but now it was too late. Currently she wasn't willing to sacrifice her newfound freedom, not even for love.

Georgina realized she'd misjudged Langston's reaction to turning down his suggestion they live together when he'd send her funny emojis to begin and end her day. He'd called to inform her they would be leaving the Falls to drive to DC late Friday afternoon. The Fourth of July fell on a Monday, which indicated the three-day celebration would begin Saturday morning.

Red, white and blue bunting and American flags were in abundance in the downtown business district. There was an excitement in the air that was almost palpable as a caravan of trunks with carnival rides, games and food vendors arrived to set up in a field that had been left undeveloped to accommodate the number of carnival trailers and the increasing number of vehicles belonging to out-of-towners willing to pay the parking fee.

Georgina was spending more time at the shop when, after several trips, she had transported all the bins from her house to the store. She wanted to be ready when the shelving was finally installed. She'd placed labeled removable adhesive tape on the tiled floor where she wanted the furniture arranged.

The bell rang and she peered through the solar shades. A shriek of excitement escaped her when she unlocked the door and reached for her cousin's hand. "Please come in before folks realize I'm still not open." The words were barely off her tongue when Sutton Reed picked her up and spun her around and around.

Sutton's large, dark eyes were filled with amusement. "I still can't believe that my little cousin is going into business for herself."

She kissed his smooth-shaven cheek. "Believe it. And when did you get in?"

"Less than a half an hour ago. Aunt Evelyn told me I could probably find you here."

Georgina stared at the man who had women waiting at stadium doors and in hotel lobbies to get him to notice them. His brown complexion with shades ranging from rosewood to alizarin, and features, which appeared almost too delicate for a man, were qualifications for Sutton when he'd appeared in People magazine in their most beautiful issue. And seeing him up close and personal was a testament to that description. Whenever he looked at someone, they seemed mesmerized by eyes that gave them his full, undivided attention, and with his towering height and muscled physique he was an imposing figure.

"I can't believe you're no longer on house arrest."

Georgina narrowed her eyes at him. "That's not funny."

Sutton reached for her, but she managed to avoid him. "I'm sorry, Georgi. That was uncalled for. I know how long you've wanted to move out on your own."

She crossed her arms under her breasts. "What's the saying? Better late than never. Enough about me. How's your knee?" He'd shattered his right knee sliding into a base, and was subsequently placed on the injured list. Sutton underwent a serious of surgeries, and then notified his agent that as a free agent he was retiring from the game.

Sutton ran a hand over the stubble on his recently

shaved pate. "It's a barometer. It tells me every time we're going to have inclement weather."

"How long has it been since your last surgery?"

"Seven months followed by countless weeks of rehab. At thirty-six I'm too old for baseball and too young to retire and sit back to do nothing. I'm going to wait a year before I decide what I want to do with the rest of my life. Meanwhile, I plan to do what I can to help out at the store."

"Did your mother come up with you?"

Sutton rolled his eyes upward. "She called at the last minute to tell me she was staying in Atlanta for the holiday. I didn't want to ask because I knew I wouldn't like the answer about who or what is keeping her there."

"Do you think she's still seeing your father?"

"I don't know and don't want to know." He glanced around the space. "You really picked a nice place."

"I was lucky because the landlord completely renovated it after the last tenant. He put in a new floor, updated the electrical system and modernized the bathroom. You can have a look around if you want."

"I'll do that at some other time. I just stopped in to let you know I'm back. Are you going to need help setting up?"

"I don't believe so. The deliverymen will set up the furniture, and those bringing the shelving know they have to anchor them to the wall."

"What about a security system?"

Georgina smiled. It was one of the first things her father had questioned her about once she went over the details of setting up shop. "I'm waiting for him to arrive within the hour." Once she stored her inventory, two flat screens and two sewing machines in the storeroom, she'd scheduled a date for the entire premises to be wired directly to the sheriff's office.

Sutton tugged on the braid falling down her back. "Good for you. I know you're busy, so I'm looking forward to seeing you over the weekend."

"I'm not going to be here for the weekend. I have to go to DC on business." Georgina had decided not to say anything to her family about becoming a children's book illustrator until she'd agreed to the terms in her contract. And she decided not to sign anything until she had her lawyer look it over."

"Well, I suppose I'll see you when you get back."

She looped her arm through Sutton's. "Of course you will. Now that you're staying with your uncle and auntie, I will be certain to drop by and see how you're adjusting to life in a small town."

Since moving out, Georgina stopped in to see her parents once and no more than twice each week, while her mother called every other day to give her an update of the goings-on in the store. She knew Evelyn missed her, and Georgina had to admit she missed seeing her mother, yet decided now that the cord was cut, she did not want to revert to the time when Evelyn depended upon her for constant companionship.

"You forget I came from a small town, and I must admit it feels good to be back."

"Are you saying you got tired of Hot Lanta?"

"Don't get me wrong, Georgi. I loved Atlanta, but there were times when I just wanted to walk out of my house and encounter absolute silence. I didn't need to hear planes flying overhead, car tires on the roadway, or even my closest neighbor's music whenever they were having a party. Wickham Falls isn't Mayberry, but it comes close. I know times have changed where we now have folks addicted to drugs, but it still hasn't reached the stage where it's become an issue."

"That's true. The Falls has changed, but not so much that it has diminished the quality of life," she said in defense of their hometown.

Sutton tugged on her braid again as he lowered his head and kissed her forehead. "I'm proud of you, Georgi, for going out on your own. If you need anything—and I mean anything—just let me know and I'll help you out."

She laughed. "You're no different than my father. Thank you very much, but I don't need any money, Sutton."

He winked at her. "Just asking."

The ringing of the bell chimed throughout the empty space. "That must be the technician."

Sutton walked to the door. "I'll hang out here until he's finished."

"That won't be necessary."

"I'm not going to leave you alone in here with some strange man who may use it as an opportunity to take advantage of you."

"Are you still watching those crime shows?" she asked as he walked to the door. Sutton had admitted to her that his guilty pleasure was watching true-crime programming.

"I wouldn't miss them," he said over his shoulder, and then unlocked the door.

The technician walked in, holding out his ID badge. "Yo, man. You're Sutton Reed. I remember that triple play you made when you caught that fly ball, stepped on first base to double up the runner and then threw home to cut down the player at the plate."

Georgina sat, sighing when Sutton and the technician launched into a discussion about baseball. Her cousin was prepared to leave before she'd mentioned someone coming to wire the store, and now he was deep in conversation with a man whose knowledge of baseball indicated he was an avid fan of the game. West Virginia did not have a professional baseball team, but that didn't keep folks in the Falls from rooting for either the Washington Nationals or the Atlanta Braves. Rather than sit and listen to the two men talk sports, Georgina retreated to the storeroom and opened a large bin with knitted and crocheted babies', toddlers' and children's hats, sweaters and socks. Whenever she sat long enough to relax, she found herself knitting and crocheting handmade garments she anonymously donated to the church's outreach for their clothing drive. She didn't know why, but she always became emotional when seeing a child wearing one of her creations.

Georgina managed to crochet and finish two beanies using lime-green baby yarn by the time the technician completed his task. He'd installed cameras and sensors before instructing her step by step how to arm and disarm the system. He promised to return to hook up a panic button under the reception desk once her furniture was delivered. She waited for Sutton and the technician to leave before punching in her code, arming the system, to leave and return home to pack for her trip to DC.

Georgina stared out the windshield when Langston came to a complete stop in the driveway leading to his sister's home. The three-story house was dark, and she wondered if Jacklyn was still up.

"Maybe we should've waited for tomorrow morning to drive up. It looks as if everyone has gone to bed." They'd left Wickham Falls at nine because Langston wanted to wait for the latest edition of *The Sentinel* to come back from the printer.

Langston undid his seat belt. "Jackie's still up.

She claims she's more creative once everyone goes to bed."

"What if she isn't up?"

"Stop stressing, babe. I called my sister before I came to pick you up, so she knows to expect us."

Georgina undid her seat belt and waited for Langston to come around to help her down. She was looking forward to seeing his sister again, if only to reminiscence about high school. There were times when she regretted not attending college because then her social circle would have expanded beyond the kids with whom she'd gone to high school. Langston had formed friendships with his college roommates and colleagues at the television station, while her day-to-day existence did not venture beyond the environs of Wickham Falls.

Langston had helped her out and gathered their bags from the cargo area when the front door opened. "See. I told you Jackie would still be up."

She walked with Langston up the porch steps, smiling when Jacklyn extended her arms. "Thank you for inviting me to your home."

"There's no need to thank me, Georgi. You're involved with my brother, so that makes you family."

Georgina wanted to tell Jacklyn that she was getting ahead of herself. She and Langston sleeping together did not translate into an engagement or even marriage. "We'd wanted to get here earlier but—"

"Don't you dare apologize," Jacklyn said, cutting

her off. "I rarely get to bed before one in the morning. The exception is when Peter's home."

"Is your husband going to be here this weekend?"

"He came in a couple of hours ago. Whenever Peter is called away, I never know for how long or when he's coming back." Jacklyn looped her arm through Georgina's. "Come inside. I'll show you guys to your room. I'm going to put you in the mother-in-law suite where you will have complete privacy, because it's off-limits for the kids."

"How old are your children, Jackie?"

"Brett is five, and Sophia is three going on thirty-three. Both are really excited because they're going to spend a couple of weeks with my parents on their houseboat."

"Are you going with them?"

"Nope. It isn't often I get a break from my kids, so when Mom and Dad asked to see their grandkids I did not hesitate to say yes. Peter's on vacation, so he's going down with them. Once you have children, you'll discover that a temporary break is needed to maintain your sanity."

Georgina wanted to tell Langston's sister that at thirty-two she still had time before she began thinking about starting a family, because at the present time it wasn't a priority for her.

Jacklyn led them down a hallway off a sitting room. "You guys are here." She opened a door and stood aside while Georgina and Langston walked in. "Sleep well."

Georgina smiled at Langston once Jacklyn had closed the door behind her. The suite to which they'd been assigned had a king-size bed, sitting area, double dresser, en-suite bath and walk-in closets. "This is very nice."

"Jackie thinks of you as special, because whenever I come to visit, I always sleep in one of the third-story bedrooms."

"You're just her brother, while I'm going to be her illustrator."

Langston set their bags on the floor in a corner. "Bragging, princess?"

"Yes." She slipped out of her tennis shoes and then unbuttoned her blouse. "I don't know about you, but I'm ready to go to bed—to *sleep*," she added, when he flashed a wolfish grin.

"Aw, baby. You're not going to give me some?"

"No, and not for the next five days."

He stared at her before realization dawned. "Oh, I see."

Even if she hadn't been on her menses, Georgina had no intention of allowing Langston to make love to her in his sister's home. She wasn't being prudish but felt what they did to and with each other could be done in the privacy of either of their homes.

Bending, she opened her weekender and removed

a nightgown and a cosmetic case. "If you don't mind, I'm going to use the bathroom first."

Fifteen minutes later she reemerged to find Langston in bed, snoring lightly. It was apparent he hadn't waited for her. She slipped into bed next to him and turned off the bedside lamp. Resting an arm over his flat belly, she closed her eyes and fell asleep.

Chapter Thirteen

Georgina sat in the Lindemanns' home office with Amelia Kincaid. The room was more like a living room than an office with a sofa, chairs, wall-mounted flat screen, audio equipment and a wood-burning fireplace with family photographs lining the mantelpiece.

The fifty-something woman had arrived from New York on the noon train, and Peter Lindemann had volunteered to drive to Union Station with his son and daughter to pick up his wife's literary agent. Jacklyn said every time her husband returned home from an assignment his children treated him like Santa on Christmas morning.

When Georgina was introduced as their uncle

Lang's friend, Brett and Sophia had cautiously approached her before Sophia crawled up on Georgina's lap to ask to touch her hair. The toddler appeared transfixed that she had curls like her uncle's friend. Both children had inherited their father's dark-blond hair, and their hazel eyes were a strikingly beautiful contrast to their light brown complexion.

Georgina felt slightly uncomfortable as Amelia continued to stare at her but vowed not to let the other woman see how much she was affected by her. Amelia took off her tinted glasses and pinched the bridge of her pencil-thin, narrow nose. Sunlight coming from the window behind glinted off short, jet-black hair, reminding Georgina of a crow's or raven's feathers.

"You're quite a surprise, Georgina."

She gave the older woman a direct stare. "Why would you say that?"

"When I first saw your illustrations, I thought you would be a lot older."

Georgina's expression did not change. The woman was not only rude but also judgmental. "Are you saying that my age is going to be a factor when it comes to negotiating a contract for me?"

Spots of color dotted Amelia's fair complexion with the jab. "Not at all. I'm just saying that you will probably enjoy a long and celebrated career as a children's book illustrator once I convince Jacklyn's publisher that you should become her personal one."

Georgina lowered her eyes. "I'm sorry. Forgive me for being presumptuous."

Amelia laughed. "Not only are you beautiful, but also modest."

Jacklyn cleared her throat. She'd held her twisted hair off her face with a wide headband. "My brother would definitely agree with you, because he and Georgina are in a serious relationship."

Realization then dawned as to why Amelia had appeared so entranced with her. It was apparent the agent was attracted to women, and it was the first time she'd become conscious of someone of the same sex seemingly coming on to her.

"By the way, where is your brother?" Amelia asked Jacklyn.

"He left to go to the television station where he used to work to reconnect with some of his former colleagues."

Appearing satisfied with Jacklyn's explanation, Amelia opened a leather binder filled with a sheath of papers. "Well, I think it's time we get down to discussing business." She unscrewed the top to a fountain pen and scribbled something. She tore off the page and handed it to Georgina. "This is what I'm going to ask them to give you for the first book in the series."

Georgina stared at the numbers. "Is this your highest, mid or lowest quote?"

Amelia slumped back against the cushion on the armchair and put on her glasses. "Why are you asking?"

"Because it seems quite generous for a first-time illustrator. I know the more they offer me the higher your fee as my agent. What I don't want to do is price myself out of contention when the publisher feels they can get someone for a lot less."

"It is on the higher end of the scale," Amelia admitted.

Although she did not want to minimize the worth of her talent, Georgina also wasn't going to let the agent make it impossible down the road for her to sell her sketches. "What if we start at the middle, then when it comes time to negotiate for a subsequent contract we can ask for a little more than the higher end of the scale?"

Amelia's mouth tightened in frustration. "Your illustrations definitely warrant a little more, Georgina. Do you have any idea of how talented you are? You are truly a gifted artist."

She gave the avaricious agent a long, penetrating stare. "I am aware of my talent because my grandmother told me a long time ago that I have a special gift. So yes, I know that I'm talented." Georgina pointed to Amelia's pad. "Perhaps you can write down another figure that would make it easier for me to agree to have you rep me." The agent scribbled another number and this time Georgina smiled. "That's better. Once the contract is finalized I'd like my attorney to go over it before I sign and send it back to you."

Amelia retuned her smile. "Did you major in business in college?"

"No. I never went to college, but I did have the best teacher when it came to running a business. My father."

"She's right," Jacklyn confirmed. "The Powells have owned and operated the same family business in Wickham Falls, West Virginia, since right after the Civil War, so she's definitely not a novice."

Georgina realized Amelia now saw her differently. If the woman's client had been anyone other than Jacklyn, Georgina would've walked out of the meeting. Greed bred contempt, and she wanted no part of it.

"I will draw up a contract between you and me, outlining my fee and the length of the agreement, which can be terminated in writing with thirty days' prior notice. I hope this meets with your approval?"

Georgina nodded. "It does."

Amelia stood up. "I'm going to go to my room and work on this."

Waiting until the woman left, Jacklyn closed and locked the door behind her and sat on the love seat next to Georgina. "You really pissed her off. There aren't too many who are able to challenge Amelia Kincaid, who has earned a reputation as a piranha. It's true she fights to get the most money out of a publisher for her clients, but she's also in it to make as much for herself. She's never married, doesn't have any kids and lives in a prewar, rent-controlled apartment on the Upper West Side overlooking Central Park that belonged to her parents, and she's also as penny-pinching as they come. Whenever she entertains a client she always orders the cheapest item on the menu."

"Aren't those expenses tax-deductible?"

"Yes, but she still doesn't like to spend money. The one time she came down to meet with me I'd discovered that she'd checked into a flophouse and wound up with bedbug bites. That's why I tell her she can stay here."

"How do you think she would react if you gave her a bill for lodging and food?"

"You know you're bad, Georgina Powell," Jacklyn teased as she flashed a wide grin. "Enough about Miss Tight Wad. Now you have to tell me how you and my brother got together."

Georgina told her everything from the time she and Langston shared a table and a dance at the Chamber fund-raiser, to his being supportive when she decided to move out and start up her own business.

"Are you aware that my brother is in love with you?"

Georgina stared at the pattern on the rug. "I am, because he told me."

"Are we talking about the same Langston Wayne Cooper? Because even when he told me he was going to marry Ayanna, he refused to admit that he was in love with her."

This revelation about the man she had fallen in love with shocked Georgina, because not only was he forthcoming about how he felt about her, but he held nothing back whenever they made love. "Maybe he's changed because of what he'd experienced as a foreign correspondent. Being bombarded daily with the possibility of death can be very sobering."

Jacklyn squeezed her hand. "It's apparent you know my brother better than I do. I promised Peter I would cook out if doesn't rain. He's probably going to invite some of his buddies from the Bureau along with their wives to come over and hang out with us this weekend. So I'm going to warn you in advance that there's going to be a lot of testosterone and concealed weapons in attendance, which I insist they lock up as soon as they arrive."

Georgina laughed and wanted to remind Jacklyn that there probably wasn't a house in the Falls where there wasn't a rifle, shotgun or handgun. Her father had taught her to shoot the year she turned twelve, and the recoil from the powerful automatic nearly knocked her off her feet. It took weeks of practice before she was able to load, unload and hit a target. Then she swore never to pick up a gun again.

Langston felt Georgina's pride as if it was his own. It was her grand opening and A Stitch at a Time was filled with curious and potential customers. Although she had had to wait until the second week in July to open, the wait was more than worth it.

The town council did not meet during the months of July and August; however, several members were on hand to cover the event while Jonas Harper was in attendance to take photos for the newspaper.

Once they'd returned from Washington, DC, Langston did not get to see Georgina as often as he would've liked. And it was as if time had sped up because she was spending more time at the shop waiting for the delivery of furniture and accessories, and then meticulously stocking the Plexiglas shelving with yarns and threads by color and weight. He was in awe when he saw an entire wall of colors from alabaster white to midnight, unaware there were that many colors in the spectrum. He also learned that quilting squares were called fat quarters, crochet hooks were sized by letters and knitting needles by numbers.

She'd arranged the space for ultimate relaxation with love seats and armchairs, where one could opt to watch television or indulge in coffee from a single-serve coffeemaker, an assortment of teas and a cooler with dispensers for hot and cold water. Georgina had ordered an assortment of cupcakes and pastries from Sasha's Sweet Shoppe for the occasion. Framed prints of women knitting, crocheting and quilting adorned the walls covered in a pale wheat-like fabric. There were signs advertising free instructions with purchase of materials, a display case with hats, sweaters, scarves and afghans for sale. Also a corner table with sewing machines and racks from which hung hand- and machine-made quilts. The shop also had a customer-only restroom.

Georgina had designed an ad with a coupon offering escalating discounts for total purchases, and even deeper discounts for the first twenty customers. Her logo, a quilt square along with the shop's address and telephone number, was stamped on white paper shopping bags and business cards.

Langston had interviewed her for the "Who's Who" column and planned to run it in the upcoming edition along with Jonas's photos. When she initially told him she wanted to host her grand opening on a Sunday he'd thought it odd, but when Georgina explained that she wanted people to stroll in and look around and possibly sign up for instruction and then take several days to determine if they wanted to join the scheduled classes she'd set up, he realized it was a brilliant plan, because her first official day of operation wouldn't be until Tuesday.

Georgina's parents and Sutton had also stopped by. Evelyn appeared to be overcome with emotion when she walked in and saw that all the time and hard work her daughter had put into A Stitch at a Time to make it a charming retreat where her customers could come to develop and explore their creativity. He'd found it almost impossible not to stare at Georgina as she exchanged pleasantries or showed someone a pattern from one of the many instruction books on display. Langston had teased her when she'd shown him the black smock with white lettering identifying the business, that she'd turned in Powell's for Stitch's. She'd laughed, and then explained as an artist she had to represent the medium because she remembered having to wear a smock whenever her classes went to art.

There were times when Langston forgot that she was an artist whether sketching her illustrations or piecing a quilt. He'd visited museums where there were exhibits with quilts and other textiles. He had come out to report on her grand opening, but also to support the woman with whom he wanted to spend the rest of his life. The first time he'd asked her to move in with him Langston knew it had been too early in their relationship to make that request. Her comeback that she wasn't raised to shack up with a man spoke volumes. She wouldn't live with him unless they were married.

And he did want to get married again, and hopefully get it right the next time. But he had to remind himself that Georgina wasn't Ayanna. She didn't have abandonment issues and had come into her own as an independent woman and business owner, while he didn't have a career that would take him away from home for extended periods of time. Langston knew he had to wait, wait until Georgina felt confident enough to manage her career, marriage and hopefully children. He'd watched her interact with his niece and nephew, and Sophia clung to her like Velcro. She followed Georgina everywhere and cried when she set her down. Even his sister had mentioned her daughter's fixation with his girlfriend, teasing him that he shouldn't wait too long to make Georgi an auntie for her children.

Waiting until there was a lull in foot traffic, Langston approached Georgina and kissed her cheek. "You are incredible. Congratulations."

Eyes shimmering with excitement, Georgina smiled up at him. "Thank you for helping me set up everything."

"There's no need to thank me, Georgi. I love you and would do whatever I can to make certain you succeed in whatever you set out to do."

She lowered her eyes. "Don't, Langston."

"Don't what? Don't love you?"

Georgina sucked in a breath to compose herself. It wasn't what he'd said, but how it had come out. The passion in his voice made her heart stop for a few seconds before starting up again. All before they were just words, but this time they were more. And for the first time since coming face-to-face with him at the fund-raiser she realized how much he did love her.

"We'll talk about this later. Once I close up, I'll come by your place. I'm not opening until Tuesday, so maybe I can convince my man to take a few hours off on Monday so we can spend some quality time together."

Langston shrugged his shoulders. "I don't know if that's possible. I have to ask my boss if I can take time off."

"You are the boss, Langston."

His expressive black eyebrows lifted. "You're right. I am the boss."

Rising on tiptoe, she brushed a kiss over his mouth. "I'll see you later."

"Okay, sweets."

Georgina watched him walk, unaware her mother was staring at her. "You really like him, don't you?" Evelyn whispered in her ear.

"I love him, Mom."

Evelyn looped their arms. "What are you going to do about it?"

She turned and stared at Evelyn, who looked nothing like the woman she was before she'd gone to Hawaii with her husband. She'd regained some of the weight she'd lost over the years, her hair was fuller, styled in a fashionable bob, the chemically straightened strands ending at her jawline.

"What do you mean?"

"Are you going to marry him, or are you going to drag your feet and let some other woman sink her hooks in him?"

"Mama. Langston and I haven't been dating long enough to even broach the subject of marriage."

"You're not a girl, Georgina, but a grown-ass woman with a ticking biological clock. If not now, then when?"

Georgina could not believe what she was hearing. In the past it had been her father talking about grandchildren, and it was apparent her mother had become his ally. "I'm not going to answer that. I don't intend to fast-forward my relationship with Langston because you want to become a grandmother. However, if things change between us you will be the first one to know."

Evelyn pressed a kiss to her temple. "Thank you, sweetheart. I know I don't say it enough, but I'm so proud of you. This place is beautiful. I know my mother was disappointed that I didn't like knitting or crocheting, but I think it's time I pick it up again. Maybe I'll make Bruce a sweater for Christmas."

"I recommend you begin with an afghan. I have patterns where you can crochet and complete one in forty-eight hours."

Evelyn smiled. "That sounds more like it."

"I know your favorite colors, so I'll pick out the yarn and photocopy a few patterns that will work up quickly."

"Thank you, baby."

Minutes before five, Georgina turned over the sign on the front door from Open to Closed, lowered the solar shades covering the plate-glass windows and dimmed the recessed lights. She cleaned up the coffee station, ran the vacuum cleaner over the floor and carpeted area and rearranged chairs. Potted plants and vases of flowers from well-wishers covered the surface of a table next to the reception area. Her grand opening wasn't about ringing up sales but a welcoming event to introduce townsfolk to their newest local business.

Georgina lay in bed with Langston, holding hands. Within minutes of his opening the door to her ring, he'd swept her up in his embrace and carried her to the bedroom where he'd undressed her and entered her body without saying a word. Words were irrelevant when they allowed their bodies to speak for them.

And she knew at that moment if he'd asked her to live with him, Georgina would've ignored what her mother and grandmother had preached to her about shacking up with a man. She was modern woman who didn't need a promise of marriage to live with a man.

"I think I'm going to ask my boss to take a few hours off tomorrow," Langston teased.

She turned to stare at his profile. "Who will cover the office?"

"Now that Sharon is away, Randall is next in line."

"When did she quit?"

"She didn't quit, princess. She took a leave to deal with some personal business."

"I remember when I used to go the paper's office to hand in an ad or drop off a check, Miss Sharon would give me what I thought of as the stink-eye, because the woman never smiled."

"Sharon is all business and the life's blood backbone of the paper. It would've gone under a long time ago if not for her."

"You've done wonders with *The Sentinel*. It was on life support before you took over and folks were saying it was just a matter of time before it folded completely."

Langston gave her hand a gentle squeeze. "It hasn't been an easy journey, and everyone is on board to keep the presses rolling."

Georgina pressed her face against his muscular shoulder. "You don't have to take off. I'm going to be here all day tomorrow and plan to make a special dinner for you when you come home."

"Be careful because I can be spoiled quite easily with just a few homemade dinners."

Releasing his hand, she straddled his body. "Get used to it, my prince. Because spoiling you makes me very, very happy."

Georgina could not have envisioned the pace in which her business had taken off. She had a steady stream of customers signing up for lessons and more experienced ones who came in to sit and work on their projects, or form new friendships.

The summer was over and with waning daylight hours and the approaching fall and winter holidays, many knitting and crocheting projects were quick sellers. A month following her meeting Amelia, the agent forwarded her the contract from the publisher, which she gave to Nicole Campos-Austen for her perusal. The local attorney gave her a thumbs-up, congratulating her on her new venture. Georgina signed the contract and now awaited an executed copy and payment, which would legally make her a professional illustrator.

Georgina had knitted a birthday sweater for Langston's nephew using a royal blue acrylic yarn. The front of the garment had orange pumpkins, a haystack, scarecrow and cornstalks. She'd resisted knitting witches or other ghoulish images because she felt they weren't appropriate for a child to advertise. Jacklyn had called to tell her Brett did the happy dance when he saw the sweater and refused to take it off even when it was time for him to go to bed.

Georgina leaned over the woman attempting to piece squares using the sewing machine. "You have to control the speed, or your stitches will be uneven."

Mrs. Jefferies shook her head in exasperation. "I just can't use these newfangled machines. I'm so used to quilting by hand."

"Then you should continue to quilt by hand, Mrs.

Jefferies. It may take longer, but you have more control."

The older woman's eyelids fluttered. "I want to finish this crib blanket for my new great-grandbaby for Christmas."

Georgina patted her shoulder. "Don't stress yourself. I'll machine stitch the squares for you, then you can finish it up by hand."

"Really?"

She smiled. "Yes. I'll call you when I'm finished."

The octogenarian gave her a warm smile. "Thank you so much, Georgina. You truly are a blessing."

She thought it was the opposite. Her customers were a blessing for her. They patronized her shop more than they had the crafts section at Powell's. She'd believed she had enough inventory on hand to last at least six months, but swift sales were an indicator she would have to reorder sooner rather than later.

Her relationship with Langston had grown even stronger and there were times when she spent more nights at his house than at hers. Many of the homes in the new development on the Remington property were completed, and Georgina had to decide whether she would continue to rent the guesthouse, move in with Langston, or put in a bid to purchase one of the newly built homes.

She'd lowered the shade in preparation of closing when her cell phone rang. "Hi, Jackie."

"Hi, yourself. Amelia dropped by to leave our executed contracts and checks. I told her to mail yours to you, but I assume she didn't want to pay the postage to overnight it. I can't understand her. She said we live close enough so you can pick it up from me. I just can't get over her obsession with hoarding money."

"It takes all kinds to run the world, Jackie. Maybe she had a partner who took advantage of her generosity where she was left almost penniless, and that's scary for someone who has to depend on themselves to stay afloat."

"I never thought of that. I know I can mail them to you, but the kids have been asking about you."

Georgina smiled. "I miss them, too. I close Sundays and Mondays, so I'll let you know when I'm going to drive up to see them. Don't tell them I'm coming because I want it to be a surprise." Her surprise would be to give both knitted hats and scarves from a supply she had on hand for sale.

It was the first Wednesday in December and Langston was scheduled to attend the monthly town hall meeting, and knowing she would find him at his office, she decided to stop by to give him her good news before going home. She locked up, walked around the corner to Main Street and mounted the staircase to the second story to *The Sentinel's* office.

The door was unlocked, and she walked past the reception area to Langston's private office, stopping short when she heard him talking to someone. Her eyes grew wide when she did not want to believe what she'd overheard.

"Yes, Mom. I do need the money and I'm going to ask her for what I need to cover the year-end salary increases and bonuses. Why are you trying to talk me out of it? I wouldn't ask if I didn't have a problem with cash flow, but this is going to be a one-time request. Yes, I know she's going to go off on me, but she'll get over it because we love each other."

Georgina had heard enough. She retraced her steps and practically ran down the staircase and out into the night. A cool mist feathered over her face like a gossamer spider web and when she brushed her cheek her fingers were moist from the tears flowing down her face.

Not again! screamed the silent voice in her head. For the second time in her life she'd fallen in love with a man who'd used her for his own selfish purposes. She hadn't told Langston how much she was paid for the illustrations; he was aware that she'd set up her shop without taking out a business loan; and he was also cognizant that as a new business, A Stitch at a Time was doing well.

She drove home, filled the bathtub with bath salts and sat in the nearly scalding hot water and willed her mind blank until the water cooled. Then she did something that she'd never done before. She drank several glasses of wine and then crawled into bed and slept until dawn.

Georgina waited until she knew Langston would be up to call him. He answered after the second ring. "Good morning, princess."

"Langston, I've decided I can no longer see you."

"What!"

"Something has come up in life that won't permit me to become involved with a man. Goodbye."

Chapter Fourteen

Langston felt as if he'd been kicked in the head. Georgina's phone call had left him shocked and numb for days. His first impulse was to walk around the corner to her shop and demand she talk to him but didn't want to cause a scene, which no doubt would impact her business.

He spent days and nights searching his memory as to what he may have said to turn her off but could not come up with a plausible explanation for why she'd decided to break up with him.

She's pregnant! It was the only thing he could think of to elicit her abrupt change in behavior. They'd made love once without using protection, and he'd made her promise to tell him if she was pregnant. He didn't want to think she was carrying his child and rather than trap him she'd elected to absolve him of all blame for not using a condom.

Pressing his head against the back of the executive chair, Langston decided to wait and give her time to come around. If they'd had an argument or disagreement, he would've understood her wanting to break off with him. He loved Georgina and knowing she wasn't going anywhere made his decision to wait more satisfying.

Georgina handed Jacklyn her jacket, picked up Sophia and rubbed their noses together. "How big is my favorite girl?" She'd called Jacklyn to let her know she'd planned to come to Alexandria the weekend before Thanksgiving.

Sophia raised her arms above her head. "This big, Auntie Gigi." She looked over the child's head and met Jacklyn's eyes.

"That's what they call you, Georgi. And when are you going to make that a reality?"

She set the child on her feet. "What are you talking about?"

"We need to talk. Sophia, Momma and Auntie Gigi have to talk so I need you to go and play with your dolls."

Sophia stomped her foot. "I don't want to play with my dolls! I want Auntie Gigi."

"What's going on here?" Peter asked as he suddenly appeared out of nowhere. Georgina stared at the tall, imposing agent with a military haircut. His face was deeply tanned, which made his green eyes much more vibrant. "What did I tell you, Sophia, about talking back to your mother?"

"She won't let me stay with Auntie Gigi."

Peter picked up his daughter. "Your mother and auntie have business to discuss that does not include something little girls need to hear."

Jacklyn mouthed a thank you to her husband. She'd told Georgina that she met her future husband when she'd attended Howard University. She was an undergraduate while he was enrolled in Howard Law. He graduated, applied to the FBI and a year later they were married.

"Come into my office where we can have complete privacy."

Georgina sat and glanced around the office. Jacklyn had lit a fire in the fireplace. "I love this room. It's like a warm hug."

Jacklyn smiled. "It's my favorite room in the entire house. I tell Peter that I don't need to go on vacation because this space is my sanctuary."

"You have a wonderful family."

A beat passed. "Thank you. And I hope beyond hope that you would also become part of my family."

Georgina knew it was time for her to open up to Langston's sister as to why she decided to break up with her brother. "Langston and I are no longer seeing each other." Jacklyn's jaw dropped with this disclosure. It was apparent he hadn't told her that they had split up. She continued revealing what she'd overheard Langston talking to his mother about, asking her for money, despite his pronouncement that he did not need it. "I dated a man who had a gambling addiction and strung me along for eight months with the intent of using mc to bail him out. Do you realize why I refused to date anyone in high school?" Jacklyn shook her head. "It was because I heard boys talking about going out with me because my father owned the department store and I stood to inherit everything once he retired or passed away."

"You eavesdropped on a conversation where you only heard one side?"

Georgina knew Jacklyn was angry when her hands tightened into fists. "I'd heard enough."

"For someone who's so incredibly talented, you are just as naive. Don't you dare open your mouth to defend yourself until I have my say, Georgina Powell. Langston would never need your money because he has a net worth of seven figures. I minored in finance and he's trusted me with his investments. The advance and royalty payments from Langston's books made him a very wealthy man. He had me run the figures before he bought the newspaper and the house from our parents where we were raised. He was talking to our mother about asking me to withdraw money from one of his accounts to cover year-end raises for his employees. And that should be a lesson to you about jumping to conclusions without hearing both sides of a conversation."

Georgina placed a trembling hand over her mouth. She'd misjudged the only man whom she wanted to marry and have children with. "I'm sorry, Jackie."

"Don't tell me, Georgi. You need to call Lang and apologize to him."

Reaching into the back pocket of her jeans, she took out her phone and tapped his number. "Yes, Georgina."

"I'm sorry."

"Where are you?"

"I'm in Alexandria with your sister."

"How long do you plan to be there?"

"Long enough for you to get here."

"Hang up. I'm on my way."

Georgina sat on a bench at the rear of the Lindemann property, baring her soul to Langston. "I'm sorry I misjudged you. Can you forgive me?"

Reaching for her hand, Langston massaged the back of it with his thumb. "I'll have to think about it but on one condition."

"What's that?"

"Marry me, Georgina Powell. Marry me and make me the happiest man in the world."

Resting her head on his shoulder, she cried without making a sound. "Yes, I will marry you," she whispered. "When?"

Shifting to face her, Langston anchored a hand under her chin and kissed the tears dotting her cheeks. "I'll leave that up to you. I'd like to give you a ring for Christmas, but it's your call when it comes to setting a wedding date."

Georgina placed light kisses at the corners of his strong mouth. "I'd like a Valentine's Day wedding."

"Will it fall on a weekend?"

"I don't care, as long as I become your wife on the day set aside for lovers."

Angling his head, Langston gave her a long, healing kiss, sealing her promise and their future. "Let's go inside and give everyone the good news."

"I'm certain Sophia is going be ecstatic when I try to explain to her that she's going to be Auntie Gigi's flower girl."

Georgina said a silent prayer of gratitude that she'd gotten a second chance at love with a man who'd come back to Wickham Falls to start over and begin a new life with her.

* * * * *

#2767 THE TEXAN'S BABY BOMBSHELL
The Fortunes of Texas: Rambling Rose • by Allison Leigh
When Laurel Hudson is found—alive but with amnesia—no one is more relieved than Adam Fortune. He will do whatever it takes to reunite mother and son, even if it means a road trip in extremely close quarters. Will the long journey home remind Laurel how much they truly share?

#2768 COMING TO A CROSSROADS
Matchmaking Mamas • by Marie Ferrarella
When the Matchmaking Mamas recommend Dr. Ethan O'Neil as a potential ride-share customer to Liz Bellamy, it's a win-win financial situation. Yet the handsome doctor isn't her usual fare. Kind, witty and emotionally guarded, Ethan thinks love walked out years ago, until his unlikely connection with his beautiful, hardworking chauffeur.

#2769 THEIR NINE-MONTH SURPRISE
Sutter Creek, Montana • by Laurel Greer
Returning from vacation, veterinary tech Lachlan Reid is shocked—the woman he's been dreaming about for months is on his doorstep, pregnant. Lachlan has always wanted to be a dad and works tirelessly to make Marisol see his commitment. But can he convince marriage-shy Marisol to form the family of their dreams?

#2770 HER SAVANNAH SURPRISE
The Savannah Sisters • by Nancy Robards Thompson
Kate Clark's Vegas wedding trip wasn't for *her* wedding. But she still got a husband! Aidan Quindlin broke her heart in high school. And if she's not careful, the tempting single dad could do it again. Annulment is the only way to protect herself. Then she learns she's pregnant...

#2771 THE SECRET BETWEEN THEM
The Culhanes of Cedar River • by Helen Lacey
After months of nursing her father back to health, artist Leah Culhane is finally focusing on her work again. But her longtime crush on Sean O'Sullivan is hard to forget. Sean has come home but is clearly keeping secrets from everyone, even his family. So why does he find himself wanting to bare his soul—and his heart—to Leah?

#2772 THE COWBOY'S CLAIM
Tillbridge Stables • by Nina Crespo
Chloe Daniels is determined to land the role of a lifetime. Even if she's terrified to get on a horse! And the last thing her reluctant teacher, Tristan Tillbridge, wants is to entertain a pampered actress. But the enigmatic cowboy soon discovers that Chloe's as genuine as she is gorgeous. Will this unlikely pair discover that the sparks between them are anything but an act?

HSECNM0520

When Laurel Hudson is found—alive but with amnesia—no one is more relieved than Adam Fortune. He will do whatever it takes to reunite mother and son, even if it means a road trip in extremely close quarters. Will the long journey home remind Laurel how much they truly share?

Read on for a sneak preview of the final book in The Fortunes of Texas: Rambling Rose continuity, The Texan's Baby Bombshell *by Allison Leigh.*

He'd been falling for her from the very beginning. But that kiss had sealed the deal for him.

Now that glossy oak-barrel hair slid over her shoulder as Laurel's head turned and she looked his way.

His step faltered.

Her eyes were the same stunning shade of blue they'd always been. Her perfectly heart-shaped face was pale and delicate looking even without the pink scar on her forehead between her eyebrows.

Her eyebrows pulled together as their eyes met.

Remember me.

Remember us.

The words—unwanted and unexpected—pulsed through him, drowning out the splitting headache and the aching back and the impatience, the relief and the pain.

Then she blinked those incredible eyes of hers and he realized there was a flush on her cheeks and she was chewing at the corner of her lips. In contrast to her delicate features, her lips were just as full and pouty as they'd always been.

Kissing them had been an adventure in and of itself.

He pushed the pointless memory out of his head and then had to shove his hands in the pockets of his jeans because they were actually shaking.

"Hi." Puny first word to say to the woman who'd made a wreck out of him.

Still seated, she looked up at him. "Hi." She sounded breathless. "It's…it's Adam, right?"

The pain sitting in the pit of his stomach then had nothing to do with anything except her. He yanked his right hand from his pocket and held it out. "Adam Fortune."

She looked uncertain, then slowly settled her hand into his.

Unlike Dr. Granger's firm, brief clasp, Laurel's touch felt chilled and tentative. And it lingered. "I'm Lisa."

God help him. He was not strong enough for this.

Don't miss
The Texan's Baby Bombshell *by Allison Leigh,*
available June 2020 wherever
Harlequin Special Edition books and ebooks are sold.

Harlequin.com

Don't miss the second book in the Wild River series by

Jennifer Snow

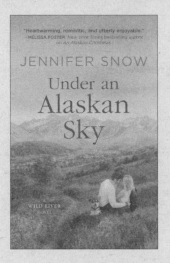

"Never too late to join the growing ranks of Jennifer Snow fans."
—*Fresh Fiction*

Order your copy today!

Be sure to connect with us at:

Harlequin.com/Newsletters
Facebook.com/HarlequinBooks
Twitter.com/HQNBooks

HQNBooks.com

SPECIAL EXCERPT FROM

HQN

Keep reading for a special preview of
Under an Alaskan Sky,
the second book in Jennifer Snow's
sizzling Wild River series.

Cassie and Tank are the ultimate will-they-or-won't-
they couple. Just when it seems like that might change,
Tank's ex arrives in town…

Coming May 2020 from HQN Books!

Tank ripped his invite in half.

"What are you doing?"

He frowned. "We're not actually going to the party…are we?"

Cassie nodded slowly. "I think I will…"

Tank reached for the tape on her desk. "Guess I should have clarified that first."

Cassie smiled. "You don't have to go."

"Of course I do if you're going. I told you. I'm here. For support." He taped the invite. "We will go together."

Together. Of course they'd go together. They did everything together. Unfortunately, she knew enough not to think of it as a real date. "Great," she said.

If Tank could sense it wasn't actually great, he didn't show it. "Are you coming to Kaia's soccer game today?"

She nodded. "I'll be there. I hope it's a different ref this time. That call against her in the last game was bullshit."

Tank raised an eyebrow. "So that's where she got it."

"Got what?"

"The potty mouth," Tank said with a grin.

Cassie felt her cheeks flush. Okay, so maybe she wasn't always the best influence on the little girl. Which was one of the reasons why Tank doubted her ability to be in Kaia's life full-time. She wanted to prove to him that she could handle the responsibility of being a caregiver to Kaia…but she refused to change who she was. "Sorry about that."

Tank waved it off, but his expression grew serious. "Hey…has Kaia mentioned anything about her mom to you?"

Cassie frowned, her heart racing at the mention of Tank's ex. He never brought her up. Like, ever. "No… She showed me the unicorn stuffie she sent for her birthday, but she hasn't said much else. Why do you ask?"

Tank shoved his hands in his pockets and rocked back on his heels. "No reason. They've just been Skyping lately and I… Never mind. I'm sure everything's fine."

They're Skyping now? The last Cassie had heard, they spoke several times a year at most. Birthday gifts…Christmas gifts. She didn't know the full story, but Tank and his ex had agreed that was for the best. Apparently, Kaia's mother had decided to change their arrangement. Cassie could tell by Tank's expression, it hadn't been his idea. "Do you want me to ask her about it?"

Tank shook his head. "No. I'm sure she will talk to me about it when she's ready." He headed toward the door.

Funny, that's what Cassie always thought about Tank. In five years of friendship, he'd barely mentioned Kaia's mom. From what Cassie had gathered, Kaia kept in contact, but Tank had no relationship with his ex. They didn't need to. They weren't sharing custody of Kaia or having to coparent.

But Tank's silence regarding their history had always spoken volumes. Cassie suspected there was a good reason Tank was worried about this increasing contact between his daughter and her mother now.

Would he ever open up about it?

He hesitated at the door, but then opened it. "I'll see you at the game," he said as he left the store.

Obviously not today.

Under an Alaskan Sky *by Jennifer Snow.*

Look for it May 2020 from HQN Books!

HQNBooks.com

PHJSEXP0520